"Stop Fighting Me," He Whispered.

"All I ask from you tonight is the truth, or at least a portion of it."

"What portion?" she asked, already aware of the warmth of him as he overwhelmed her senses.

"At least admit that you want me! Just stop fighting me long enough to let me show you how good it will be between us."

He held her wrists in one hand above her head, letting his fingertips trail sensuously down the length of her throat.

"After tonight," he muttered, "you will play your games with no one else. I'm going to make sure you know the limits of the golden chains. . . ."

STEPHANIE JAMES
readily admits that the chief influence on her writing is her "lifelong addiction to romantic daydreaming." She has spent the last nine years living and working with her engineer husband in a wide variety of places including the Caribbean, the Southeast, and the Pacific Northwest. Ms. James currently resides in California.

Dear Reader,

Silhouette Special Editions are an exciting new line of contemporary romances from Silhouette Books. Special Editions are written specifically for our readers who want a story with heightened romantic tension.

Special Editions have all the elements you've enjoyed in Silhouette Romances and *more*. These stories concentrate on romance in a longer, more realistic and sophisticated way, and they feature greater sensual detail.

I hope you enjoy this book and all the wonderful romances from Silhouette. We welcome any suggestions or comments and invite you to write to us at the address below.

Karen Solem
Editor-in-Chief
Silhouette Books
P.O. Box 769
New York, N. Y. 10019

STEPHANIE JAMES
Stormy Challenge

Silhouette Special Edition

Published by Silhouette Books New York

America's Publisher of Contemporary Romance

Other Silhouette Books by Stephanie James

A Passionate Business
Dangerous Magic
Corporate Affair

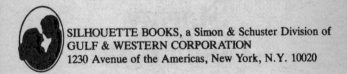

SILHOUETTE BOOKS, a Simon & Schuster Division of
GULF & WESTERN CORPORATION
1230 Avenue of the Americas, New York, N.Y. 10020

Copyright © 1982 by Jayne Ann Krentz

Distributed by Pocket Books

ISBN: 0-671-53535-8

First Silhouette Books printing July, 1982

10 9 8 7 6 5 4 3 2 1

All of the characters in this book are fictitious. Any resem-
blance to actual persons, living or dead, is purely coincidental.

Map by Tony Ferrara

SILHOUETTE, SILHOUETTE SPECIAL EDITION
and colophon are trademarks of Simon & Schuster.

America's Publisher of Contemporary Romance

Printed in the U.S.A.

Stormy Challenge

OREGON AND
CALIFORNIA

Chapter One

*L*ater, she would ask herself how she could possibly have missed all the danger signals emanating from the man. With the inevitable wisdom of hindsight, she would feel the lazy menace in him as clearly as she now felt her own deeply intrigued response, and Leya Brandon would wonder bitterly why her normally astute mind and intuition had betrayed her.

It was to be only the second time in all her twenty-seven years that she had allowed herself to be so misled by a man, but Leya would take little comfort from that fact. She rarely needed a second lesson in anything.

But for the moment, on the dance floor of the secluded inn on the wild Oregon coast, Leya wasn't thinking of the future. The man held her in such an intimate dancing embrace that she was obliged to rest both hands on his broad shoulders. The way he shaped the curve of her waist made it impossible to concentrate on anything but the present. Leya tipped back her neat head, the long, sable-dark braid falling dramatically over one shoulder and across her breast, and smiled up into Court Gannon's sensuously narrowed tortoiseshell eyes. The look she met in the gold-flecked gaze caused her fingertips to flex ever so slightly against the subtly rough texture of his jacket.

The inviting, waiting look in Court's eyes deepened as he felt the small movement on his shoulders.

"You feel like a kitten trying to decide whether or not to settle in for the night," he murmured in soft amusement, turning his head slightly to touch her wrist with his lips. It was the lightest, most teasing of caresses, yet Leya was aware of the small shiver which coursed through her.

"Not for the night," she made herself answer, with a smiling ease that took a surprising amount of effort. The realization that it was going to be difficult to refuse Court's imminent invitation to share his bed hit her with some force. My God, she thought wonderingly, I've only known him two days! "But a few more dances would be welcomed," she concluded softly.

"It will be my pleasure to provide the dances," he growled in his dark, heavily shaded voice. "But I warn you I intend to use the time to my own advantage." The large, strong hands at Leya's waist tightened meaningfully and the golden brown eyes gleamed.

Leya's full, generous mouth curved a fraction more as she regarded her partner from beneath thick eyelashes. "Coming from someone who doesn't believe in exerting himself unnecessarily, that sounds rather energetic," she observed teasingly.

"The operative word is unnecessarily," he drawled. "And I'm coming to the conclusion that having you for an entire night is going to be very necessary, indeed!"

Leya felt the warmth flood her face even as she tried to retain her normally abundant common sense. "There's a certain lack of subtlety in your approach tonight," she accused chidingly as she sought for a light way of handling the increasing sensual tension between them.

"I've had the impression from the beginning that the usual games weren't going to be necessary between us, Leya," Court retorted almost gently, his eyes searching her features for the truth of her feelings toward him.

"It's not a question of playing games, Court," she replied, the smallest of frowns drawing her dark brows slightly toward each other. "It's a matter of being sure. Why does a man imply a woman is teasing or playing games when she is only trying to test the depths of her own reactions and those of the male involved?"

"Because he's horribly afraid that if he allows the woman to probe her feelings too deeply, she'll talk herself out of going to bed with him!" Court said and grinned candidly.

"So he deliberately tries to make her feel guilty by accusing her of being a tease?" Leya shot back, silver-green eyes deepening with a nonverbal rebuke.

"Exactly. Can you blame us? All's fair in love and war!"

"Situation ethics, Court? I'm surprised at you. I would have thought you were the type of man who lives by a definite set of principles," she mocked.

"And doesn't alter them to fit the situation? Well, in

a sense, you're right." He smiled unabashedly. "It's just that the principles I choose to live by are my own."

"Developed by you and for you?"

"Ummm," he agreed, his fingers kneading the contour of her lower waist with blatant pleasure.

Leya felt the pleasure in his hands as it communicated itself to her and knew she was going to have difficulty when it came time to say goodnight. She refused to think of how difficult it would be when the moment for good-bye came, as it would in only a few short days.

But vacation romances, however pleasant, were doomed to appallingly short lives, she told herself firmly. They were meant to be enjoyed on a superficial level and then forgotten—light flirtations that could be ended without serious regret. For Leya, that meant not having to live with the knowledge that she had given herself casually to a man who wouldn't remember her name by the time his next vacation arrived.

But regardless of what happened between them, Leya knew she wouldn't forget Court Gannon's name for a long, long time. Nor would she forget anything else about the man with the tortoiseshell eyes and matching hair. Large and solidly built without being an ounce overweight, he topped six feet by about one inch, she estimated and she found pleasure in the way his wide shoulders narrowed into a lean waist and strong thighs.

There was power in this man, and Leya was honest enough to admit it attracted her. Only later would she tell herself she should have been wary of that primitive attraction. But the mastery and strength were cloaked in what was, for Leya, an enormously appealing laziness and self-control.

The variegated deep gold and dark brown of his thick hair was cut short in an apparent effort to tame the broad wave that threatened to fall across his wide forehead. More than once, Leya had been forced to exercise a degree of control in order to restrain herself from reaching up to thrust curious, sensitive fingers through the curve of that hair. She knew her own weakness for tactile sensations and deliberately avoided the temptation.

Heavy brows and long lashes shielded the well-spaced and deep-set brown-and-gold eyes. A bold, no-nonsense hand had chiseled Court's face, leaving an aggressive nose and an unconsciously arrogant tilt to the strong chin. Broad, jagged planes that left no room for soft handsomeness marked the high cheekbones and tightly fleshed skin beneath. The column of his neck was strong and browned in the same sun-colored shade as his face and hands. The tan was an excellent foil for the crisp whiteness of his shirt collar and cuffs. Leya flexed her fingers once again, enjoying the texture of his richly woven wool jacket. He wore the close-fitting slacks and coat with an ease that suggested expensive if conservative tailoring.

Leya had no notion why she had looked up from the book in her lap yesterday morning to find Court Gannon watching her from across the heavily beamed and elegantly rustic lobby of the inn. She had responded automatically to the mildly prickling sensation of being observed and lifted her head to meet the unexpected impact of the gold-marked eyes. The moment she had acknowledged his presence, he had started forward with a deliberate, lazy stride that brought him inevitably to where she curled in the corner of the old Victorian couch in front of the roaring fire. There had been a few other people seated nearby and she had told herself he was heading for one of them until it became apparent she was the focus of his attention.

A little uneasily she had listened to his brief, polite introduction as he seated himself beside her, stretching out long legs toward the huge stone fireplace which dominated that end of the room. The initial unease had been natural enough, given the fact that Leya had no illusions about being an eye-catching beauty.

The truth of the matter was that she thought of herself as rather average. An average five-and-a-half feet in height, an average, perhaps overly rounded figure that required an average amount of dieting and an average, attractive set of features. She knew full well she had above-average intelligence and sense of humor but she didn't really expect most men to notice or appreciate those two virtues. Especially not clear across the lobby!

In spite of her own dismissing assessment of her looks, more than one man in the past had been attracted by the very un-average and unusual combination of long, sable-brown hair with the strange silvery green of her eyes. The effect was a subtle one and not usually noticed consciously at first, but it was there. It allowed Leya to wear the strong, bold colors she favored. Her features were feminine but not soft. They betrayed the intelligence and self-awareness lying underneath, as well as the strength those two factors ensured. Her firm chin, straight nose, and perceptive eyes were gentled a bit by long lashes and the ready curve of her mouth.

No, not a great beauty, Leya had told herself wryly, and dressed as she was yesterday in well-washed jeans and a brilliant burnt-orange velour top, it was natural enough to wonder why a stranger had picked her out of the crowd. Of course, she had added in silent amusement, the crowd was very small. It was winter, the summer tourists were long gone, and not everyone favored the fiercely rugged southern Oregon coastline at this time of year. Only those with a penchant for the intriguing wildness of a storm over the sea or the mystery of a fog-shrouded stretch of beach came at this time of the year. They felt themselves amply rewarded.

"What are you thinking about?" Court broke into her thoughts to demand suddenly, the rather hard line of his mouth quirking at the corner as he studied the flicker of thought in her eyes.

"Yesterday," she admitted simply.

"What about yesterday?" he persisted softly, using his hands to press her more intimately against his hard leanness. He was using the dance as an excuse to make love to her, Leya realized with a small sense of shock. She felt her pulse quicken in response to the barely disguised arousal in him.

"The way you came toward me through the lobby as if you knew me." She smiled. "I was afraid you were someone I should know, whose name I couldn't remember!"

"You were right," he told her meaningfully. "I was someone you should know. The only reason you couldn't remember my name was because I hadn't given it to you yet."

"That opening conversational gambit of telling me the ending of the novel I was reading was clever, too." Leya grinned cheerfully. "It ruined my plans for the entire day, since I had intended to spend the whole of it reading that book!"

"I wanted you free to spend the time with me."

"So I gathered," she said dryly. "But it wouldn't have worked if you hadn't turned out to be every bit as lazy and uninterested in tennis as I am!"

"Oh, I knew we were two of a kind from the moment I spotted you across the lobby," he assured her humorously, the laughter reaching his eyes and warming them nicely. "Let's face it, only a certain type of person is going to come here at this time of the year."

"Someone who has no aspirations to be the next tennis star or golf hero?" she quipped, aware that the music was drawing to a close.

"Someone," he told her deeply as he took her arm and guided her back to the small table, "who understands that walking along a beach at dawn is life's only important sport!"

"I'm afraid my dedication to the ideal falls somewhat short," she murmured ruefully as she took the seat he held for her. "I have to admit to finding dancing a very interesting alternative. And for someone who claims to be too lazy to do anything except walk for exercise, you do a pretty good job on the dance floor!"

"But dancing with you isn't a form of exercise," he pointed out, lifting the glass snifter in front of him and taking a man-sized swallow of the potent cognac.

"No?" Leya inquired, arching one brow with a hint of warning.

"No," he confirmed, heedless of her faintly quelling expression. "It's a prelude to making love to you, and I would never," he added in a soft rasp, leaning forward to watch the color in her face, "make the mistake of classifying sex with you as a sport or a game!"

"Court!" Leya snapped, determined to let him know that he had stepped too far out of bounds. "That's enough on the subject. You wouldn't want me to think you have a one-track mind, would you?" She made an effort to inject a caustic note into the small setdown she had attempted to deliver. But it was difficult to maintain that faint air of outrage beneath the glittering light in his eyes. Her real reaction to his blatantly sexual talk was an unfamiliar weakness that left her feeling pursued. Leya Brandon was not accustomed to the role of hunted female. And, she promised herself silently, she did not intend to allow this man to treat her as prey. She was glad he found her attractive because the feeling was mutual, but she had very definite ideas on equality in a relationship. She also had very definite ideas on the depressing nature of relationships based purely on sex. The last thought firmed her mouth and Court was far too observant not to have seen the faint hardening in her silvery green eyes as well.

"A one-track mind is exactly what I seem to be developing around you, Leya," he confided with a sensual twist of his lips. "Do you know what my first thought was this morning?"

"What?" she asked warily, reaching for her own snifter and sipping delicately. In the candlelight the deep emerald color of her long-sleeved gown glowed. The light reflected warmly from the unusual green pendant set in gold that hung in the deep opening of the dress.

"I thought that it was all wrong I should be waking up alone. You should have been there with me," he whispered, with such intensity that Leya blinked uncertainly.

"I've told you the conversation has gone far enough," she breathed, forcing her willpower to the fore. It was not a characteristic in which she normally found herself deficient. "I suggest we either switch to another topic or say goodnight."

"You don't like knowing that I want you?" he queried whimsically. "Or are you afraid of admitting that you want me, too?"

"If you think you're going to trap me into answering a double-edged sword of a question like that, you're considerably less intelligent than I originally believed you to be!" she informed him loftily, forcing back the rush of laughter she was experiencing.

"It was worth a try." He shrugged with massive resignation, an answering grin in his eyes. "Well, what would you like to discuss? I'm at your service, I assure you. At least until I can think of a way to steer the conversation back to my main interests!"

"Limited though those interests appear to be?" she mocked.

"There's nothing limited about them," he informed her kindly. "You're just jealous because I know how to establish priorities and stick to them!"

Leya flung up a hand in laughing self-defense. "Enough! I'm going to choose a topic and you're going to do me the courtesy of following my lead!"

Court lounged back in his leather-padded chair and

smiled benignly. "You leave me little choice. I am, after all, wearing the clothes of a gentleman tonight."

"And you always suit your actions to your clothes?"

"Not always, but as a special favor to you tonight, I'll make the effort. That is until the clock strikes twelve," he concluded with a theatrical salute of his snifter.

"You have a pumpkin waiting to take you back to your room at midnight?" Leya asked interestedly, leaning forward to prop her elbow on the table and rest her chin on her palm. The green stone at her throat gleamed softly in the light; a gleam that was reflected in her eyes. She smiled.

"Don't worry," he told her. "There's room for two inside."

"About my conversational topic," she began determinedly.

"Yes."

"Have you had a chance to read that contract my brother wants me to sign, so that he can go ahead and hire this high-powered consultant he's found?" Leya plunged into the question that had been on her mind ever since she'd given the papers to Court for his opinion.

"I've read it. I went through it before I picked you up for dinner," he admitted quietly, a new note of seriousness entering the heavy-timbred voice. Across the table, the tortoiseshell eyes met hers.

"Well?" she pressed a bit grimly. "Do you agree with me?"

"That it's dangerous? It could be in the wrong circumstances," Court said slowly, evenly. The cognac swirled gently in his glass.

"I knew it!" Leya stated with unhappy satisfaction.

"As soon as Keith gave it to me I knew there was something crazy about the whole setup!"

"I said it could be dangerous in the wrong situation," Court repeated calmly, watching her face closely. "You were wise to be cautious, Leya, but there are some mitigating circumstances involved here."

"Such as?" she challenged.

"Such as the fact that you know your brother, and I know the other party named in the contract. The man he wants to hire."

"You know him!" Leya stared, totally astonished by this information. "You know this C. Tremayne? But how could you? Where would you have run into him?"

"In Silicon Valley," he told her, using the slang expression for the area around San Jose, California, where so much of the new high-technology electronics industry was based. It had been so named for the semiconducting material that had helped revolutionize solid-state electronics.

"You worked down there for a while?" Leya demanded, confused. "I didn't know you were in engineering. I thought you said something about finance. . . ."

"I've worked with several electronics firms, helping them secure venture capital. It takes money to do first-class research and I help them find it," he said, as if it were the simplest thing in the world.

Leya knew there was a lot more to it than he implied, but she had other things to pursue at the moment. "So you've met Tremayne? What do you think of him?"

Court smiled. "He's not the ogre you've convinced yourself he is, for a start."

"He must be!" Leya scoffed. "What sort of creature besides an ogre would try to tie my brother to a contract like the one I gave you to read?"

"A man who has as much to lose as your brother and wants to protect himself as well as his client," Court explained tersely.

"All the protection is on Tremayne's side!" Leya exploded in disgust. "The way that contract is written, he's tied his salary into the profits. If my brother's company does well, Tremayne stands to make a tidy sum, far more than a normal salary for consulting!"

"And if Brandon Security Systems goes under, Tremayne loses said fortune."

"What about that business of insisting on full decision-making authority?" Leya persisted irritably. "He's virtually setting himself up as president of the firm!"

"From what I know of him, Tremayne doesn't make decisions by consensus," Court admitted dryly. "He wouldn't go into a situation like this unless he had the power to do what needed to be done, without having to refer everything to a committee."

"But the main reason Keith insists on having the man in as a sort of chief consultant is because he's hoping to learn from Tremayne! If Tremayne won't be bothered with discussing his decisions, what good will that do Keith?"

"If Tremayne has agreed to guide your brother over the next couple of years, until Keith has enough experience under his belt to take on the full responsibility of running the firm, you can rest assured he'll do as he says. In my experience, Tremayne is a man of his word. He just wants it clear from the outset that for the duration of the contract, he's in charge. If you ask me, your brother is showing a lot of sense. After all, it must be damned intimidating to suddenly inherit a large business at the age of twenty-five. You did say he was a couple of years younger than you?"

Leya nodded morosely. "I realize he's had no experience in running the firm. After all, everyone assumed Dad would be in charge for years. . . ." Grimly, she turned her thoughts away from the sudden death of her parents the previous year in a plane crash in Europe. She and Keith had both put the grieving behind them. Coming to grips with the present was the important thing now.

"From what you've told me, your brother never really had any intention of taking over the reins," Court noted quietly, his eyes probing.

"No. It came as a complete surprise when he decided to assume the responsibility instead of just selling out," Leya admitted. "He seems a new man lately, as if he's found himself." She shook her head, thinking of the way her brother had been drifting since graduation from college. "That's why I hate to put the squelch on this idea he has of apprenticing himself to Tremayne, but . . ."

"But you're afraid he's agreeing to a contract that will ruin him?" Court concluded understandingly.

"You read it. It's rather binding, wouldn't you agree?" Leya retorted brusquely, running her finger idly around the rim of her snifter and watching the play of candlelight on the liqueur inside.

"Yes, but your brother's interests are well protected,

Leya. Don't forget, you still hold half the firm's shares in your power. If Tremayne proves dangerous, it wouldn't be impossible to fire him. All you'd have to do is to get Keith to agree he'd made a mistake. The contract is only truly binding as long as all parties are satisfied. Keith is just asking for a chance to do things his way. Are you sure you're not playing the part of the overprotective big sister?"

Leya lifted her eyes, the metallic green gaze narrowing in response to the small accusation. "No," she snapped. "I'm exercising my obligations as co-owner of the firm. The agreement Tremayne wants signed needs both my signature and my brother's. My father left Brandon Security to both of us!"

"With the understanding that for the most part you would be a silent partner, you said," Court reminded her gently but firmly.

Leya winced. "I may have told you a little too much of the background of this deal before I asked your advice," she grumbled, annoyed with herself.

But it had been so easy to talk to Court last night. She was still amazed at the relaxed and communicative atmosphere that had sprung up between them from the start. One thing had led to another and before she knew it she had been discussing the main reason she had secluded herself at the inn for a week. She had promised Keith a decision on whether or not to hire Tremayne by the time she returned to Santa Rosa, the town in northern California where she made her home and ran her book business.

Court smiled. "I think your basic decision isn't whether or not to sign the contract, it's whether or not you're going to let your brother really assume control of the firm."

Leya gritted her teeth, forcing herself to consider the justification of his comments. "I have never been a bossy older sister!"

"You strike me as the type of woman who could get quite bossy," he chuckled.

"Except that I'm too smart to make that mistake with my own brother. I don't want him to hate me!"

"How about with a lover? Would you make the mistake of trying to dominate a man in a relationship?" Court pounced provocatively, sitting forward with a deliberate air. The gold-flecked eyes glittered with teasing challenge.

Leya smiled with serene superiority, aware of the heat in her veins. "That's different," she demurred. "Everyone knows a man is happiest in a relationship when he's properly managed."

"Funny, I always heard it was women who were content when they'd been mastered!" Court purred.

"A myth," she responded breezily. "Fostered by all those old Rudolph Valentino movies featuring sheiks who carried their women off into the desert!"

"Not to mention all those other films featuring masterful types such as Gable and Bogart and . . ."

"So Hollywood got off on the wrong track," Leya retorted, lifting one nearly bare shoulder dismissingly. "Most of the films were made by men, so it stands to reason they emphasized male fantasies."

"That theory doesn't explain all the women in the audiences." Court grinned.

"Who can ever account for an audience reaction?"

"Who can ever account for a woman's reaction?" he countered.

"I stand by my theory," Leya declared, removing her chin from her palm and settling back into her chair. "And I have *not* been a domineering older sister!"

"Then why break a precedent and start behaving like one now?"

Leya took a deep breath. "You really think I ought to go ahead and let Keith hire Tremayne?" For the life of her she couldn't explain why she should value this man's advice. But some instinct said he knew what he was talking about. There was a sense of sureness and authority about Court Gannon that made itself felt. You had the feeling that he knew what he was doing and his advice would be solid.

"Yes. You asked for my advice and I'm giving it. I think you ought to sign and let your brother get on with the business of learning how to run the company he's inherited, which you don't particularly want. He sounds like a young man who's found what he wants to do in life. Let him do it. Not all of us are that lucky at twenty-five!" he added with a wry smile.

"Sad but true," Leya sighed, shaking her head with an answering smile. Her own most depressing memories of thinking she knew what she wanted were from her twenty-sixth year. Well, she had learned her lesson. There was no point in rehashing the subject. Her smile widened deliberately as she considered the man across from her. "Did you know where you were going and what you wanted when you were twenty-five?" Privately, she put his present age at around thirty-five or thirty-six.

Surprisingly, he paused to consider the question. "In some aspects of my life I was quite certain of what I wanted," he finally said slowly.

"You sound as if you're trying to hedge the question," she accused softly.

"A man's privilege," he shot back easily, eyes laughing. Then he went on in a careful tone. "I guess the truth is I knew what I wanted as far as my career was concerned, but there were until quite recently some very open-ended questions about what I wanted in my personal life."

Across the table, Leya caught the sudden blaze of intensity in him, and a part of her wanted to turn and run. The flash of cowardice was so unexpected she found herself swallowing in nervousness. It took an astonishing amount of self-control merely to stay seated and force a deliberately unconcerned expression.

"I don't see you as the unsure type," she confessed lightly.

He looked as if he were about to pursue the statement and then appeared to change his mind. "Tell me something," he said instead, eyeing her. "If you had so many qualms about signing this contract, why didn't you make it a point to meet with this C. Tremayne and judge him for yourself?"

Leya blinked at the change of topic and then lifted a negligent hand. "If you must know, I chose this particular week for a vacation because Keith informed me Tremayne was trying to set up just such a meeting. I felt . . ." she broke off, searching for the right word, "as if I were being pushed. The man didn't handle it very politely, you see. He simply told my brother to bring me to the office on a certain day and time this week, and he would handle me." She grimaced in mild displeasure.

"So you immediately disappeared on vacation?" One heavy brow lifted.

"I told Keith I'd take the contract with me and make up my mind while I was away," she explained, aware that she was tapping one foot gently under the table. She had the impression Court was about to condemn her for failing to go through with the meeting, and Leya didn't appreciate the prospect of criticism from him.

"I can see you think you know what I'm going to say next," he teased. "But you're wrong."

"Am I?"

"Yes. I'm not going to tell you that you should have stayed and had the meeting with Tremayne."

"Why not?" she demanded dryly, positive that was what he was thinking.

"Because I'm too happy to have you sitting across from me tonight," he retorted smoothly. "I'm very glad you're here and not back in Santa Rosa!"

Instantly, Leya relaxed, her lips curving warmly and the silvery green glance softening. "So am I," she agreed gently.

"And I wouldn't have wanted to forgo this encounter for all the semiconductors in California," he finished, voice thickening with male anticipation, an ancient, primitive anticipation that had the power to send answering shivers of alarm and excitement through her.

"Thank you," she whispered, trying to sound only as if she were responding to a polite compliment.

"You're welcome," he growled in soft laughter. "Are you ready to come up to my room now?"

Some of the silver in Leya's eyes coalesced into a harder substance, even while her heart picked up a beat. "Your subtlety is slipping again."

He smiled with only a touch of the predator. In fact, an onlooker would need to be quite alert to notice the implication of the flashing teeth because the heat in the golden eyes was so overpowering. "You have to come up to my room," he said patiently.

"Why?" she demanded starkly.

"Because the contract is there. I left it on the table by the window."

"I'll get it in the morning," she evaded, acutely aware of the fencing match in which she was engaged. The contract was nothing more than a polite excuse for the war of wills.

"I don't want to be responsible for it overnight," Court insisted. "It represents your brother's whole future."

"You could bring it downstairs now," Leya suggested huskily, her eyes never leaving his.

"I'll compromise and bring it to your room," he announced with a totally false magnanimity that amused Leya in spite of the intriguing danger of the situation.

"Do you ever give up?" she whispered curiously.

"No." It was a simple statement of fact and she believed him. Unconsciously, Leya ran the tip of her tongue over her lower lip, tension heightening all her senses. He waited.

"You can't come to my room. Not tonight," she

finally told him quietly, her eyes meeting his in a direct, honest look.

"And you won't come to mine," he confirmed.

"I . . . I can't . . ."

"You mean you're afraid," he corrected softly.

She drew a long, steadying breath. "Perhaps." She didn't try to deny the accusation and saw him nod in satisfaction.

"I'll settle for that tonight."

"What?" she almost yelped, suddenly outraged. "You *want* me to be afraid of you?"

The sexual tension seeped out of her body to be replaced by affronted feminine anger. The green glance hardened and she watched him through suddenly narrowed lids.

"With a woman like you, I think it might be a necessary first step." Court returned her annoyed expression with one of glittering male certainty. "It ensures that I have your full attention!"

Leya stared at him, trying to decide whether to laugh or to kick him. The humorous side of her nature, nearly always in the ascendency anyway, won. She grinned recklessly.

"Are you sure you'd know what to do with my full attention once you had it? Remember, you don't approve of bossy women!"

"I am nothing if not resourceful," he assured her, rising to his feet in a smooth, coordinated movement that appealed to her notions of masculine grace. He smiled deliberately, invitingly, reaching down to take her hand and tug her gently up beside him. "And I'm perfectly willing to let you try managing me."

"Because you don't think I can do it?"

"Why don't you try it and find out for yourself how much you can get away with?" he retorted easily, leading her out of the lounge and into the main lobby of the inn.

"What would happen to your poor masculine ego if I were successful?" Leya taunted, pleasantly aware of his fingers entwined with hers as he led her through the lobby and on toward the darkened, glass-walled room which overlooked the pounding surf. The emerald dress swirled around her ankles as she moved.

"It would probably be shredded," he sighed in mock despair, guiding her through the empty, shadowy room to stand before one of its huge floor-to-ceiling windows. Below them, the wind-tossed waves crashed hugely on the rocky beach, driven by the first gales of an incoming storm. What little moonlight there was illuminated the scene in a mysterious, enchanting way. As always, Leya felt herself responding to the power of the landscape.

She felt Court's hand tighten abruptly on her fingers and knew instinctively that he was equally affected by the sensual impact of the scene. She was overwhelmingly aware that the teasing, baiting, inviting approach he had been exercising all evening had given way to something much more elemental and far more dangerous.

She also knew with intuitive self-honesty that the real danger lay in her own reactions to this man who had moved from stranger to confidant in only a couple of days. Now he was pressing his status to that of lover, and Leya told herself she must be cautious.

"We seem to have the place to ourselves. And if we sit down over there in that alcove, no one coming in will even see us. Come here, Leya," Court commanded in a low, deepening tone that pulled at her.

A moment later, Leya found herself sinking quite naturally across his knees, her head against his wide shoulder. The silver in her eyes turned to rich platinum just before his mouth covered her own.

Chapter Two

Leya's first reaction to the touch of Court's lips was that his kiss wasn't exactly what she had subconsciously expected. There was nothing tentative or uncertain about the caress and his arms held her securely enough, but there was some quality in the way his mouth played on hers that didn't fit her preconceptions. A provoking delicacy she hadn't anticipated.

Intrigued and curious with a deeply feminine curiosity, Leya wound her arms lightly around his neck, her fingertips toying with the oddly attractive gold and brown of his hair. She knew a genuine pleasure in the feel of the crisp stuff and gave a small, soundless sigh. The overall effect of the tiny escaping breath was to part her lips slightly, invitingly.

But Court made no move to take advantage of the little surrender. Instead, he continued lightly, almost teasingly to sample first the corners of her mouth and then the fullness of her lower lip. As Leya began wondering at the restraint and lack of explosion in his passion, he lifted his mouth from hers and began a fragile trail of exploration along her cheek to the edge of her lowered lashes.

Just as his lips dropped the smallest of kisses on her sensitive eyelid, his hand, which had been lying along her waist, moved. It slid upward to rest a fraction of an inch below the curve of her breast. There was a sense of impending intimacy in the touch that made Leya's pulse race.

"Oh, Court," she breathed, every nerve in her body tightening itself into a high-strung tension that was as exciting as it was uncomfortable. She felt she ought to be pushing his hand away, refusing him too many liberties, but she couldn't do that because he hadn't yet taken those liberties. So far, the depth of the intimacy was only implied.

"You look very lovely in emerald green," he offered in the softest of whispers, and the hand that had been waiting under her breast shifted once again. Leya waited for it to close possessively over the small, full curve of the green bodice, knowing she should resist when it did so. For a brief instant, she would know the feel of his hand and something in her wanted that.

But his fingers did not move to explore her breast as she had expected. Instead, he picked up the long, thick braid of sable-brown hair and toyed with it. Slowly, he lifted the length of it and drew it around her exposed, vulnerable throat, raising his head to drink in the picture she made.

"I think I know why cavemen were fond of dragging their women home by the hair. Something rather primitively sensual about the notion." The gold in Court's eyes flowed into the shadowy brown, melting it, turning it to molten amber.

Leya watched him from beneath her lashes, fiercely aware of the rope of hair around her throat. "No," she managed in faint amusement. "The ones who got dragged home by their hair were the ones who couldn't think for themselves."

"And you're much too smart to wind up in that category?" he murmured, tightening the braid ever so slightly.

"Yes." It was the simple truth.

"It isn't merely a question of intelligence, Leya," he grated, lowering his head once again to graze upon her parted lips.

"No?" she countered with amused scorn. She felt his mouth nibbling gently on hers and wanted to grab him and hold him still so that she could learn the full impact of his kiss. Her fingers tightened in the hair at the back of his head as if she would follow through with the impulse. This teasing, tantalizing string of caresses she was receiving was not enough . . .

"No." Court smiled. She could feel the smile against her mouth and wanted to use her teeth very carefully, warningly on his lower lip. But she didn't quite dare. "No," he muttered again on her mouth, "it's not just a matter of intelligence. There are some women, perhaps only one in a lifetime, that a man wants to be very sure of. One he would like to chain with golden bonds . . . !"

Leya shivered and knew he felt it. "Do you want to put golden chains on me, Court?" Her words were barely audible as she sensed the quickening of her breath and knew his fingers had released the braid to stray to her throat.

"Yes!"

There was unexpected passion in the single word, but it was not echoed in his caress, and Leya stirred restlessly against him, beginning to seek a closer touch, more of his warmth.

"I think," she murmured daringly, uncertain of her motives but knowing she wanted to provoke him a bit further, "that you have the makings of a rather possessive man."

His fingers stroked the base of her throat, drifting downward in lazy threat, and Leya shifted without conscious volition, turning into the caress, like a small cat.

"I am a very possessive man," he stated quietly. "And I will be a very possessive lover."

"When you find a woman who will let you put a chain on her?" Leya smiled in mocking challenge, watching him through slitted lashes.

"I don't plan to ask her permission," he drawled. "The chain will be in place soon enough, whether she likes it or not."

"Because you're so much smarter than she is?"

"Because I'm so much stronger and more ruthless than she is," he corrected at once. "And I've learned how to set priorities."

"You must feed that ego of yours several pounds of raw meat a day. It certainly isn't undernourished!"

Leya's eyes gleamed as she met his openly examining gaze. With her hands, she traced a path through his hair to his temples, where only the faintest hint of gray could be seen in full light. It wasn't detectable at all in the shadows tonight.

"Neither is yours," he retorted with a small grin. "You're very sure of yourself, aren't you, Leya Brandon?"

"Does that bother you?"

"Do I look bothered?" he growled, swooping gently to touch his tongue to the tip of her ear.

"No," she admitted ruefully, her eyes closing in response to his tiny caress.

"That's because I know what I'm doing, little Leya."

"And what exactly are you doing, Court?"

"Baiting my trap," he explained at once. The fingers he was using to trace patterns on her throat hovered at the green gem now.

"Are you going to explain that?" she demanded, wondering if he would touch her more intimately in a few seconds. He was so close and his hand was warm and inviting . . .

"No," he murmured cheerfully, "I'm not. There will be time enough later."

"A man of instant decision," she taunted, turning her cheek toward his questing, sampling mouth. It was all becoming too much, she thought in gathering frustration. She wanted him to touch her, try to take her by storm. She would have to halt him eventually, of course, but in that moment she longed to know the range and depth of his passion and desire. The urge to find out if he really wanted her and wasn't simply playing with her was overwhelming. What was it about this man that affected her so fiercely? She couldn't remember knowing such a physical impatience in herself before in her life. Not even when she had thought herself so much in love with Alex.

"A man who knows what he wants," Court rasped in soft agreement with her teasing assessment.

But if he truly wanted her, why wasn't he pushing and taking and demanding with his hands and his lips? Leya wondered distractedly. There had been nothing timid about his approach earlier in the evening! But, then, there was nothing particularly timid about him now, she acknowledged uncomfortably. It was this waiting, teasing, tantalizing quality in him that was frustrating. Frustrating and intriguing, she realized vaguely, her fingers sliding to the muscles of his shoulders and beginning a gentle, kneading massage.

Frustrating, intriguing, and . . . Suddenly, Leya smiled inwardly. And safe. That was the missing explanation. For all his dangerous words, he was letting her know with his body that she was safe with him. Or at least as safe as she wanted to be.

With a sigh of satisfaction at having solved the puzzle, Leya relaxed against Court's chest, deepening her own kisses as she framed his rugged face between her palms. Her self-confidence flowed serenely through her blood even as she deliberately assumed the aggressive role. The excitement was like a fire in the pit of her stomach as she kissed Court full on the mouth, probing into his warmth with the tip of her tongue. She wanted his response, needed it . . .

She felt his almost stoic resistance to the torment of

her tongue and sought to overcome it. Her body twisted against him, and her nails gently raked the side of his tanned cheek. She imagined herself in roles she'd never played: a femme fatale, a seductress, a siren.

The urgency in her grew, unchained now by any nagging, feminine fears. She was safe with this man. She could manage him. He was willing to let her set the pace . . .

"Give a woman a little taste of power . . ." Court groaned hoarsely under her soft assault, and Leya felt the reckless laughter bubble up inside herself.

"I didn't notice you giving it to me," she husked. "I thought I was taking it!" She left off the intimate duel she had initiated with his tongue and went in search of new territory to conquer. She found it in the vulnerable tip of his ear lobe. Delicately, she closed her teeth on it and was rewarded by the shudder she felt in his hard, massive frame.

"Ummm," he growled softly, his hands moving on her back as he tightened his hold slightly. "For someone who's been busy refusing my invitations to bed, you're certainly turning into a little temptress all of a sudden!"

"That's because I've finally figured you out," Leya whispered exultantly, her breath coming quickly between her parted lips as she ran her hands over the front of his shirt and played with a button or two.

"And what's the big secret?" he challenged, eyes gleaming in the darkness.

"You're not nearly so wicked as you'd have me believe," she informed him, leaning her head back and smiling at him with lazy invitation. "You said it, yourself. You're wearing the clothes of a gentleman tonight, and deep down you're going to behave like one."

"Ah," Court exclaimed as if seeing the light. "You're feeling quite safe with me now, is that it? None of the fears you almost admitted to earlier?"

"None."

"Not even a little nagging fear that you might just possibly be off in your judgment of me?" he persisted easily.

"Nope." Leya laughed very softly, her eyes glowing.

"Who am I to argue with a woman's reasoning and logic?" he murmured, lowering his head to nuzzle the cord of her throat.

"Who, indeed?" Leya quipped, wrapping her arms around his neck again and holding him close.

She plunged in where she had left off, glorying in each new response she was able to elicit from him. But with each shudder and groan and husky exclamation she drew forth from Court, there was an equally intense reaction in her own body.

The moment came when his large, powerful hand floated possessively upward to cup her breast, and instead of pushing it away as she had once thought to do, Leya made no protest. She was far too caught up in her own needs now. The wish to draw forth his male desires had unwittingly fed her own. She was aware of the touch of his fingers as they sought the nipple beneath the silky material of her dress, but her reaction was to arch against his hand, not push it aside.

"Oh!" she mouthed, feeling the tip of her breast

harden. A shudder tore through her, and she shut her eyes against the dizzying weakness that assailed her frame. The thin lace of her bra offered no protection and through the two layers of fabric, Court's fingers stirred the other nipple to life with a coaxing, seductive pattern that sent ripples of pleasure along Leya's nerves.

Her soft moans were muffled against the side of his neck as Court kissed and then nipped the exposed portion of her shoulder. She felt the touch of his teeth and dug her nails into the fabric of his jacket.

And she never quite knew when the moment came that Court actually reversed the seductive assault, making her the one under attack. One moment, Leya felt herself marvelously, supremely in command of the situation, reveling in her power; the next, she was helplessly responding to the increasing urgency in his kiss and in his hands.

She was only dimly aware that Court had suddenly captured her shaking, questing fingers as they searched for a way beneath his shirt, holding her palm to his mouth and turning his lips into it for a second before smiling beguilingly, sensuously down into her passion-filled eyes.

"I think it's time we went upstairs, darling," he whispered huskily. "This is much too public a place for what comes next!"

"Next?" she repeated, feeling idiotic, but unable to think clearly.

"I'm going to make love to you, my sweet Leya, and I want the privacy of my own bed in which to do it!"

Somehow, he got her to her feet, absorbing the

weight of her as she leaned heavily against him. With his arm supporting her around her waist, Court walked her wordlessly toward the stairs. When she turned her head to look up at him helplessly, he merely smiled with promise and undisguised desire.

Leya felt the stairs disappearing one by one beneath her feet, and a small voice in the most distant corner of her mind began yelling faintly that time was running out. Soon she would be on the landing and then in the hall outside his room . . .

How had it come to this? Leya shook her head slightly, partly in an attempt to clear it and partly in an attempt to understand what had gone wrong. She hadn't intended to go to his room tonight, she remembered that much very distinctly. No, she had kissed him because it had seemed eminently safe to kiss him. He had been restrained, gentlemanly. He had let her control the embrace, contenting himself with teasing, tantalizing caresses, which were unthreatening.

Court brought them to a halt outside his room, inserting his key into the lock, one arm still firmly around Leya. *Unthreatening,* she reminded herself grimly, as she raised her lashes to meet his eyes. The realization of what had happened hit her fully just as Court swung open the door and started to propel her gently into the room.

"No!" she breathed wryly, refusing to budge. "It's not going to be that easy, Court Gannon!"

"You mean," he soothed, swiveling to face her as she stood planted on the threshold, "it isn't going to be that easy for you to back out of it after having come this far."

"I didn't get this far on my own!" she flung back, her self-control returning in a fierce rush as the full precariousness of her situation hit her.

"No," he agreed, his mouth quirking upward. "You dragged me right along with you."

"Don't blame me for any wrong ideas you've gotten!" she declared regally, crossing her arms in front of herself and glaring at him. "All I started were a few kisses in the sitting room downstairs . . ."

"Don't you think it's time you finished what you started?" he interrupted, stepping close and curling his hand around the nape of her neck.

"There seems to be some question here of just who was seducing whom!" she stormed, feeling abused.

"Yes, but I was hoping you wouldn't realize it until tomorrow morning," he complained sadly.

"You admit you planned everything that happened? Letting me think you were going to behave like a gentleman and then allowing me to . . . to . . ." Words failed her.

"To seduce yourself and me, too? Well, yes. It seemed a simple enough plan." He shrugged.

Leya stared at him, thoroughly amused and thoroughly annoyed by the rueful expression on Court's hard features. She bit her lip and then shook her head in exasperation and sudden affection.

"Oh, Court, you idiot," she murmured softly. "I can't possibly go to bed with a man I've only known two days! After this vacation is over, we'll both be going our separate ways. I couldn't bear a casual little affair like that, don't you see? If that's really all you want or need, it would be best if we part friends tonight . . ." Her voice trailed off beneath his glittering gaze. His mouth twisted in self-mockery.

"Do you really believe that?" he whispered, the fingers behind her neck tightening. "Do you really believe all I'm after with you is a vacation fling?" He gave her the slightest of shakes.

"But, Court, what else can there be?" she exclaimed unhappily.

"As much as we want there to be, Leya," he said simply. "And speaking for myself, I want a great deal!"

"Oh, Court!"

"When you look at me like that," he muttered, "I have to believe you want there to be a great deal between us, too!"

Leya sucked in her breath, her eyes shining brighter than the gem at her throat. In the face of the emotions flaring between them, she could find nothing intelligible to say. It was too soon to hope and too late not to do exactly that. In desperation, she resorted to a bit of poor humor.

"Court, this is all so sudden," she whispered on a gurgle of laughter.

A slow smile crossed his hard face, reaching his eyes, and he tugged her close against him, letting her bury her heated face in his jacket. For a long moment, he held her that way, saying nothing at all, and she was content.

Eventually he released her, setting her a foot away and retaining a firm clasp on her shoulders while he gazed perceptively down into her questioning face.

"But no more games, Leya. We're both too old for

that sort of thing!" he said tersely, and she winced at the forcefulness in him. He meant it.

"Men seem to think anything that doesn't end in bed is a game!" she accused, making the same point, she realized, for the second time that evening.

"It is," he avowed at once.

"That's not true, Court!"

"It is for us," he said gently.

"I won't be rushed," she stated proudly, lifting her chin in automatic defiance.

"But that's exactly what I want to do," he retorted, his fingers digging almost painfully into her shoulders. "Rush you off your feet and into bed where I can make very, very sure of you."

She stepped back, out from underneath his hands, and eyed him with a mixture of speculation and longing. "You," she declared on a muffled groan, "need a good lesson in the evils of possessiveness!"

"I can't help the way I am." He refused to look apologetic. Instead, his tortoiseshell eyes seemed to be eating her.

She hesitated, feeling the undeniable pull on her senses and the equally undeniable instinct to flee while she still could. She knew she was in danger of falling in love with this man she had known so short a time, and she wanted desperately to believe he might be falling in love with her. But she must control the situation until they both were sure. With Court Gannon, she must play it safe, very, very safe . . .

Summoning a smile, she faced him with an astonishing amount of composure, under the circumstances. "Goodnight, Court. I had a very"—she paused and the smile broadened—"informative evening. Shall I see you in the morning?"

For a moment, the line of his mouth hardened, and she wondered if she was going to be allowed to escape after all. Then, he inclined his head almost formally.

"I'll pick you up for breakfast."

"Thank you. Now, as I'm here, anyway, I may as well take my brother's contract," she continued with a determined lightness. It was difficult trying to dispel the physical tension he was purposely building between them, but Leya was not without a strong will of her own.

"It's over there on the table." He watched her walk across the room and pick up the papers, a thoughtful look creasing her brow as she scanned them once more.

"Oh, hell," Leya muttered in surrender. "Have you got a pen? I might as well sign these and put my brother out of his misery!"

Wordlessly, he handed her the pen and watched intently as she flipped the pages over to the one requiring signatures. Without giving herself time to think, Leya slashed her name onto the page with a casual dash that, in a feminine way, was not unlike the equally bold scrawl on the opposite side of the paper. She glanced at the man's name once more as she tossed down the pen.

"C. Tremayne," she repeated, straightening the document and folding it into thirds. "I warn you, Court Gannon," she said with half a smile, "if that man ruins my brother's future, I'll come after you with a skinning knife!"

"You won't have far to look," he promised, a curious brightness in his eyes. "I intend to be somewhere in your vicinity!"

"You're very certain of him?" she asked quietly, the wry humor fading from her voice as she met his gaze.

"He'll deal honorably with your brother," Court stated grimly.

"Do you know anything else about him? I mean, besides his business ability?" Leya asked curiously.

"What do you want to know?" Court returned noncommittally.

Leya tapped the folded contract against her palm and considered that, eyes twinkling. "Well, is he married?"

"No. Would it matter?"

"I guess not. Merely curious."

"You know what curiosity did to the cat."

"Are you implying I shouldn't probe too deeply into C. Tremayne's personal life?" Leya grinned impishly.

"He's a man," Court tossed back with deceptive casualness, retrieving the pen.

"Ah-ha! Meaning he's a womanizer?" Leya charged brightly, enjoying the new game, especially since Court seemed rather reluctant to play. "A heavy drinker? Lots of silly macho?"

"You have got it in for the poor guy, haven't you?" Court grumbled, slanting her a disgusted look.

She sighed regretfully. "I can see I'm not going to get a lot of juicy gossip out of you! Why do men always stick together?"

"Because we have so few defenses against the female of the species. Don't worry, Leya. Tremayne will take care of Brandon Security Systems and teach your brother what he needs to know." There was a mild pause as if something had only recently occurred to Court. "You don't seem overly concerned about what Tremayne's failure to honor the spirit of the contract would do to your share of the inheritance."

"I'm not," she said carelessly, truthfully. "I have no interest in Brandon Security. I don't even know why Dad left me a portion of the shares. He knew I had all I wanted in my bookshop."

"Totally self-sufficient?" There was an amused mockery in the question.

"Completely," she confirmed, lifting one brow in a faintly quelling glance. It was the truth. She had built the shop into a successful enterprise, and she had done it on her own.

"Your father probably left you an interest in the firm so that you could act as a guardian angel for your brother in precisely such a situation as this one. He must have known Keith was not yet fully capable of handling the business," Court suggested placatingly, as if making a faint attempt to atone for his remark about self-sufficiency.

"I suppose," Leya allowed, losing interest in the matter. "Well, I'll drop this in the mail tonight so that it will go out first thing in the morning. It will get back to Santa Rosa before I do." She waved the contract briefly and started forward just as if Court weren't standing between her and the door.

But in spite of her air of determined self-confidence, Court didn't step aside. She was forced to halt in front of him, as he stood with his back to the door, his hands behind him on the knob. There was an almost grim, brooding aspect in the tightened lines at his mouth and eyes. For a moment, he said nothing, watching her as she stopped warily a few steps away.

"Court?" she tried tentatively, uncertain of his mood. Carefully, she smiled, striving for a cool, calm look, when what she secretly wanted to do was give in to a very primitive urge to run. "Is breakfast still on?"

"How long will you be staying here at the inn?" he asked, ignoring the trivial question of breakfast. He watched her as if she were a small, nervous animal he wanted to catch. Prey, Leya thought uncomfortably. He really did see her as prey. Her only defense was not to act as if she saw herself the same way!

"Five more days," she told him coolly, agreeably, as if the conversation were quite normal and hadn't taken on overtones of the sort of raw menace that can only exist between a man and a woman. The menace might be present, she thought bracingly, but so were the intervening layers of civilization. She wasn't in genuine danger. Not unless she wanted to be! She returned his watchfulness with a polite, questioning glance, her head high. "And you?"

"About the same," he returned laconically. The gold-flecked eyes went to the contract in her hand and back to her unruffled expression. His voice deepened several shades to a throaty male command that was part plea. "Stay with me tonight, Leya. Please."

"Court," she said gently, "we've already discussed this. I can't. It's just . . . too soon." Her hand moved in a helpless, ineffectual little gesture.

"You're afraid of me?" he rasped.

"Of course not!" she denied, trying to smile. She refused to think about the different aspects of fear. Not now. Now, she had to keep all her wits and self-control about her. She could do it. She knew herself to be both intelligent and strong, and she called on both qualities in full measure.

"You don't have to be afraid, Leya," he coaxed, as if she hadn't just disavowed any fear. "My trap is baited very pleasantly, I promise. You won't even hear it when the door shuts behind you."

"And in the morning?" she persisted in a distant voice, thinking that walking out of this room tonight was going to be one of the most difficult things she had ever done.

"By morning, there won't be any more talk of going back to your own bed at night!" he growled thickly, his eyes moving over her in a near-physical touch.

Leya swallowed at the sheer audacity of his words, her hand clutching the contract in a desperate, white-knuckled grip. "No," she whispered. "I need time, Court. A little more time . . ." Her words were a plea and she hated that. It wasn't like her at all!

"Time for more games?" he rapped.

"No! Time to be sure!" she flung back, growing angry. Couldn't he understand? For a long, heart-stopping moment, she wasn't at all certain he would even try to see her side of the matter, and then his lids dropped in a speculative, slitted glance. She was keenly aware of the fact that he was literally putting a tight grip on his instincts and desires. Civilization was asserting itself.

"I'll see you back to your room," he finally announced, turning to open the door. He caught her arm as she walked forward, tucking it under his in a proprietary hold.

"And then?"

"And then I'll come back here and take a cold shower!" he exploded in a muffled tone that served to lighten the atmosphere between them as nothing else could have done.

"Poor Court." She giggled as they walked down to the lobby so that she could request an envelope and stamp from the front desk. "You really did have your plans made for this evening, didn't you?"

He glanced down at her laughing, upturned face. "With my propensity for laziness, I have had to develop a talent for being organized. It's the only thing that gets someone like me through life!" His mouth twisted laconically, and the golden eyes were rueful.

"I know what you mean!" she retorted with instant honesty. "I function in the same way. I imagine there are bound to be a few problems when two people like us meet!" They stopped at the desk.

"Nothing insurmountable, I'm sure," he drawled, watching as she addressed the envelope and dropped it into the slot. She ignored his words.

"Well, that's that. Keith's day will be made when he gets the letter," Leya sighed, dusting her hands symbolically as she allowed herself to be led back up the stairs to her room.

"And now we can concentrate on the two of us," Court insisted smoothly.

At her door, he turned her briefly into his arms, his

rough, strong hands cupping her head while he examined her face. His thumbs idly worked the delicate area of her temples. "One last time, Leya, will you . . ."

"No," she cut in, smiling up at him. "The thought of you in a cold shower is too engaging to ruin!" She felt her confidence return in a warm tide, as she dug out her key. One simply had to maintain a sense of humor about life, she thought.

He shook her admonishingly, a reluctant amusement in his eyes. "For that remark, I promise you that one day you'll be joining me in a shower!" He bent down and dropped a swift, hard kiss on her mouth. "Goodnight, Leya. I'll see you first thing in the morning!" With that he was gone.

But meeting Court for breakfast wasn't quite the first thing Leya did the next morning. On the spur of the moment, she picked up the telephone after she had dressed in her jeans and a bright yellow sweater.

"Hello, Keith." She smiled into the phone. "I thought you'd like to know I signed the contract last night. It's in the mail."

"Leya!" Her brother's delighted voice came down the wire. "For that news, I'll even forgive you for having awakened me at such an ungodly hour! You won't regret it, you'll see. By the time Tremayne and I are finished, Brandon Security Systems will be number one on the West Coast!" There was a satisfied pause. "I knew once you'd met the man, you'd realize I was aware of what I was doing!"

Leya frowned uncomprehendingly. "But I haven't met the man," she began, about to tell him she'd met someone who knew Tremayne instead.

"Didn't he find you? I gave him the address of that inn. He said he would be up there in a couple of days." Keith sounded puzzled.

But puzzlement wasn't Leya's chief reaction to this piece of information. She was far too bright, too good at putting clues together to remain confused for long. It was, she thought with cold bleakness as she sat on the edge of the unmade bed, phone in hand, unfortunate that she wasn't quite bright enough to have realized what was going on before her brother dropped the clue.

"Leya?" Keith's voice prompted.

"A tall man?" she questioned dismally, already knowing the answer. "With brown-and-gold hair and eyes the color of tortoiseshell?"

Her brother laughed. "That sounds a bit dramatic, but an accurate description, I guess. I take it the two of you hit it off fairly well if he convinced you to sign that contract so quickly?"

"Oh, I have nothing but the highest admiration for your Mr. Tremayne," Leya said in soft bitterness. "An extremely clever man."

"Leya? There's nothing wrong, is there? You don't sound your usual self . . ."

The knock on the door brought Leya's head up with a sharp jerk. Her fingers tightened on the receiver. "You'll have to excuse me, Keith. Your idol has just arrived to take me to breakfast," she whispered slowly.

"Fine," Keith sang out in cheerful satisfaction. "Give Court my best, will you? Tell him I'm looking forward to working with him!"

"I'll do that," Leya promised and set the receiver back in its cradle very gently, then got up to answer the door.

Chapter Three

$\mathcal{H}$e must have known she was aware of the deception the moment she opened the door, Leya thought in cool fury. She saw the darkening of Court's eyes as he took in the set, distant expression on her face. He was every bit as smart as she was. No, that was unfair, she thought sardonically, he had just proven himself smarter. Yes, this man would know at once that he had been found out. But she wouldn't take even the smallest risk that he hadn't yet guessed.

"Good morning, Mr. Tremayne," she managed in a tight, hard voice she almost didn't recognize as her own. Her hand on the door trembled with the full force of her anger, and it took all her inner control to keep from raking the side of his face with her nails.

"Good morning, Leya," he returned quietly with such coolness that she found herself digging her nails into her palm. "I take it you couldn't resist calling your brother to tell him the good news?" he added dryly. He watched her with a hard, grim look that suggested he knew exactly what she was thinking.

She tilted her chin in chilling disdain, taking in the dark slacks that hugged his narrow hips and the maroon sweater with an open-collared cream shirt underneath. So cool, so calm, so very much the winner in their unfair skirmish. A skirmish she hadn't even guessed she was fighting.

"Congratulations," she murmured flatly. "I can only apologize that the victory was so easy for you. It must be depressing to not even get a run for your money out of your opponent. Or perhaps you prefer the easy wins?"

He reached out with one large hand and jerked the door a couple of inches, just enough to pull it free of her death grip. Automatically, she stepped back a pace as he advanced into the small room, filling it with his massiveness. He closed the door behind him with disciplined care.

"The contract," he told her bleakly, "was not the important thing between us. I wanted it out of the way."

The corner of Leya's mouth turned down in self-disgust as she faced him, the long sable braid falling across the front of her yellow sweater. She had put on boldly yellow, brightly casual earrings to go with the sweater, and their strong color was a warm note against the darkness of her sleek hair.

"I see," she flung back tersely. "For you, a victory over a woman has to be asserted in bed, is that it?" Her scorn ricocheted around the room, returning to strike again and again, but it seemed to do little damage to his tough, male hide. "For the record, when would you have told me the truth?"

"When I had you safely in bed," he admitted with such readiness that it was all she could do to keep from throwing something at him.

"You're despicable!"

"I'm practical. Done my way, things would have been a whole lot easier than they're going to be now."

"You mean you would have been more satisfied with yourself if you'd managed to seduce me as well as get my name on that contract!" she blazed. "God! What kind of man are you? To think that last night I actually thought you had something of the gentleman in you! I can't believe I've been so incredibly stupid!" She turned away, crossing her arms tightly below her breasts and walked stiffly to stand in front of the mirror over the dressing table. How could she have been such a fool? This was worse, far worse than last time . . .

He moved to stand behind her, not touching her fiercely hunched shoulders. The gold-and-brown eyes met the flaring brilliance of her silver-green gaze in the mirror.

"That's the hard part, isn't it, Leya?" he prodded knowingly. "The knowledge that you were tricked."

"Being played for a fool rarely appeals to even the most good-natured people," she shot back scathingly.

"But it's much worse for those of us who have a fairly high opinion of our own intelligence, isn't it?" he pointed out. "I told you last night I'm not the only one cursed with a healthy ego!"

Leya trembled at his words, not because of what they implied but because of what they were making her realize. It wasn't merely her ego that had been affronted by his scheming. Deep inside, she felt betrayed. And it was that feeling which was so hard to bear. It didn't help telling herself she had no reason to carry the pain that deep. The critical thing was that she must not allow him to know the full extent of the blow he had delivered.

"Rest assured," she bit out furiously, "my ego has definitely taken a beating. Perhaps that information will take the place of the seduction you seemed to need to sweeten your victory?"

In the mirror, his face tautened. "We've got a lot to talk about, Leya. Come down to the beach for a walk. I want to explain everything, honey . . ."

"You're crazy if you think I'd so much as walk down the hall with you after what you've done!" she stormed, whirling and planting her hands on her hips. "You've had all the victory you're going to get. Leave me alone!"

"I'm afraid that's not possible," he sighed.

"Would you like a little assistance from the inn manager? I'm sure he would be glad to stop you from harassing one of his guests! I'll call him!"

"Leya, calm down. I'm going to talk to you so there's no sense in ranting at me in an effort to make me leave. I'm not going anywhere without you!" There was a quiet steel in Court's voice that underlined the statement very distinctly.

"What can you possibly have to say to me? I have no wish to listen to your gloating!"

"I have no intention of taunting you about the contract, you little fool . . . !" he started heatedly.

Leya flinched at the word. "Must you call me that to my face? I'm only too well aware of my foolishness!"

"Damn it! I didn't mean it like that! It's only that I'm getting impatient with you and the phrase slipped out . . ."

"Because it's what you think I am! A fool! Well, even fools learn eventually, Court Tremayne—" She broke off with a scalding look. "What the hell is your full name, anyway? Not that it matters!"

"Courtland Gannon Tremayne," he said evenly, his mouth tight.

"As I said, it doesn't really matter!"

"Sure it does," he retorted promptly. "It's much easier to swear at someone when you know his full name!" There was the smallest hint of amusement in his face.

"You'll have to forgive my sense of humor this morning," she grated. "It's at a low ebb."

"Come down to the beach, Leya, or at least down to breakfast," he murmured coaxingly. "We have to talk."

"I'm not setting foot outside this room in your company. Can't you get it through your thick head that I don't want to see you again? You certainly seem bright enough on other matters!"

"You're determined to be stubborn about this?" he demanded in soft warning.

"Why not? It goes along with being foolish and having an oversized ego!"

"When it comes to being foolish, I'm the one who should be accepting the honors!" he snapped, putting out a hand to grasp her thick braid. With a quick tug, he forced her closer, ignoring the sharp gasp of anger and pain from his victim. "I should have kept you in my room and in my bed last night. We wouldn't be going through this little scene now if I had!"

"I can only be grateful that some remnant of my own common sense was at work last night!" she hurled back vengefully. "I can't bear to think of how much more foolish and stupid I would be feeling this morning if I had let you seduce me!"

"That's not the way it would have been. You would have understood . . ."

"If you think I would have been so awestruck by your incredible lovemaking that I would have forgiven you the deception, you're out of your mind!"

He drew a sharp breath, and she knew he was waging an inner struggle with his temper. The knowledge that she had succeeded in upsetting him to some small degree was satisfying.

"Listen to me, Leya Brandon," he charged, his grip on her hair bordering on the painful. "You're going to get the full story of how I wound up involved in this situation whether you like it or not. I would prefer to do my talking down on the beach where the breeze can evaporate some of your heat, but if you insist, I'll do it here. Take your choice. Either way, you're going to hear me out!"

"You can't force me to listen to you!" Leya wrenched her head, trying to free the braid, but she only succeeded in hurting herself.

"Want to bet? I'm a hell of a lot bigger than you are!"

"Don't you dare threaten me!" she hissed, slightly appalled at his vehemence. Why couldn't he take his victory and leave?

"I'd rather reason than threaten, but you seem beyond the reasoning point! I'm not leaving you alone until you've heard me out, Leya."

She stared at him, knowing he meant everything he said and unsure how to handle his iron will. Short of screaming, there wasn't any obvious way of getting him out of her room, and a walk on the beach didn't sound all that bad. She needed to get some of the churning anger out of her system. Perhaps she could go for the walk and let him ramble his excuses. When he'd had his say, she could simply turn her back on him. There might be some satisfaction in showing him he couldn't talk his way out of the situation. The only thing that bothered her was why he should even want to try. Unless having her signature on the contract wasn't reassuring enough for him . . .

That last thought decided her. It also jolted her. She had to remember that this wasn't just between herself and Court Tremayne. Keith was involved. And Leya still held fifty percent of the shares of Brandon Security. If she chose to try and get Keith to listen to her . . . Yes, Tremayne might have reason to be concerned.

"All right," she agreed ungraciously. "I'll go for the walk."

He relaxed visibly, releasing the chain of her braid. "Thank you, Leya."

"Don't thank me," she grumbled, turning away to collect her down jacket. "I'm going under duress. I can't understand what you're hoping to accomplish!"

"I only want to explain, that's all," he protested, watching as she zipped the front of the dark blue jacket. His eyes traveled over her with a curious possessiveness that annoyed Leya.

She said nothing as they went to his room, waiting in the hall while he picked up a sheepskin coat. He didn't try to persuade her inside, appearing to realize she'd been pushed far enough for the moment. In silence, refusing his proffered arm, she stalked beside him down the path leading to the rocky, untamed beach. The aftermath of the previous evening's storm had left the usual calling cards of carelessly tossed driftwood and broken shells. The tide was out and the sea moved sleepily under a gray sky.

Leya felt herself being absorbed into the scene, her senses responding as they always did to the feel of the ocean environment. It appealed to her love of the tactile quality in life, and when she accidentally caught Court's shrewd glance, she knew he was aware of the effect. Grimly, she closed her face so that he wouldn't start congratulating himself on that bit of perception, too!

"Well?" she prompted coldly. "Let's have it. I'd like to get the postmortem over."

He shoved his hands into the fleece-lined pockets of his jacket and shot her a narrowed glance as they walked.

"I met your brother a few months ago when he first began looking for a consultant."

Leya said nothing, her eyes fixed on the far end of the beach.

"We met initially, though, not because of my financial background but because of some work I've done with security electronics. He was interested in some of my"—Court hesitated—"some of the results of my basement tinkering."

Leya did glance up at that and as quickly away. What was it to her if he liked to work with his hands occasionally? She certainly didn't want him thinking they might have something in common!

"He was interested in exploring some of the possibilities of a gadget he found out I had put together. One thing led to another and we started talking business."

"Keith needed a consultant for the business and you needed a way of marketing your latest gadget, is that it?" Leya murmured, leaping to the obvious conclusion.

"Not quite," he shot back dryly. "There were other markets for my little security device."

"But none that offered you control of the company at the same time, I'll bet!"

"Shut up, Leya," he told her peaceably enough. "I'm trying to explain."

Leya lapsed back into silence. Didn't he realize nothing he said could possibly alter this feeling of betrayal inside her?

"Keith and I eventually reached an agreement acceptable to both of us, and then he explained about your position in the firm."

"The silent partner who wasn't being too silent!"

"But who seemed to have no interest in Brandon Security except to babysit her brother!"

Leya winced at that. Was that how Keith had taken her resistance to the idea of the contract? She had never interfered in his life before, and it was only her basic good sense that had prompted her to do so this time!

"He told me a great deal about you, honey. He's very fond of you, and he's got a lot of admiration for his independent, successful older sister. But he's found what he wants to do in life, Leya, and he's determined to do it his way. He wants you to remain the silent partner and let him run Brandon Security."

"You mean let *you* run it, don't you?" She gritted her teeth.

"I've got the experience in both electronics and finance the firm needs right now. Brandon Security is in trouble, Leya. Your brother won't be able to salvage it on his own. He's got the intelligence to see that, and he's got the guts to take the necessary steps to save it. Two years from now, he'll be a very smart, very street-wise young businessman. I'll see to that."

"We'll certainly find out if you're telling the truth, won't we?" Leya smiled with brittle, dazzling brilliance. "The contract is on its way back to Keith, and you're in charge of Brandon Security for the next two years. Bring me your report card at the end of that time and we'll see how you did!"

He came to a halt, swinging around to face her with his feet braced slightly apart. Without a word, Leya stopped, raising her cold green eyes to meet his piercing gaze.

"I don't intend to wait two years for you to forgive me, Leya."

"Why do you need my forgiveness at all?" she countered recklessly, the sea breeze loosening tendrils of dark hair and whipping them around her throat.

"Because I want you," he said with flat honesty.

Leya gaped at him in open surprise, and then her teeth closed with a snap. "Oh, come off it, Court.

Who's playing games now? You don't want me nor do you need me. Not any longer. You've gotten what you wanted!"

"No, I haven't. Not yet. But I will!"

"What you lack in romance and subtlety you certainly make up for in directness, don't you?" she mocked, outraged.

"I think," Court said slowly, examining every inch of her furious face, "that I began wanting you after your brother had told me something about you. From the way he talked, I knew I was going to find you interesting, to say the least. And I had to admire the way you'd picked up on the possible dangers in that contract we wanted you to sign. I was quite annoyed when you didn't bother to keep the appointment I'd set up for us to meet, and when I discovered you'd taken the contract and disappeared, I decided to find out for myself just what you were really like."

"So you came sneaking up here, pretending to be someone else . . ." Leya began in a voice that shook.

"I came up here to find out if the real-life woman had the same laughter and challenge in her eyes that I'd seen in the portrait in Keith's office," he drawled softly, deeply.

Leya bit her lip, remembering the portrait her father had commissioned shortly before his death and had hung in the office that was now Keith's. Then she opened her silver-green eyes very wide and spoke in liquid tones.

"Look closely, Courtland Gannon Tremayne. I'm not laughing."

He reached for her, and she stepped hurriedly back out of range, a derisive sound on her lips. Why did he continue to lie to her? It made no obvious sense! "I don't know what new game you're playing now, Court, unless you're afraid I'll turn my brother against you and make it difficult for you to do what you want with Brandon Security. But whatever it is, don't expect me to be fool enough to fall for your lies again! I know it's asking a lot in view of the current evidence, but try and credit me with some intelligence!"

"Leya, when you spontaneously asked me what I thought of that contract yesterday, the opportunity of getting it out of the way was too good to miss. But I didn't force you to sign it! You signed it because my arguments in favor of it were sound. They still are. Forget it now. That business is behind us where it should be. It had nothing to do with you and me in the first place."

Her eyes slitted at the note of urgency in his voice. "Do you really believe I'm going to simply forget what you've done to me?"

"I haven't done anything to you, damn it! Not yet, at any rate!" he growled feelingly, almost as if he were the persecuted one, Leya thought incredulously. "The contract isn't important. It was between me and your brother and should never have involved you in the first place. Naturally, I used the easiest method available of getting it out of the way . . ."

"So you could concentrate on me?" she scoffed, knowing he was lying and almost wishing he wasn't. But that was ridiculous. She wanted to be free of this man, not to discover he might actually be attracted to her after all!

"Yes!" he snapped back, frowning.

"What a waste of time," Leya said with a patently

false regret. "I'm no longer in a mood to be the focus of your undivided attention, flattering though the offer may be!"

"You didn't seem to mind last night," Court pointed out righteously. She saw his hands shift slightly at his side and knew with a sense of triumph that he wanted to grab her and shake her. If nothing else, Court Tremayne was learning he wasn't going to have everything his own way!

"Last night I thought you were someone else, though, didn't I?" Leya tossed back very sweetly. "It was a simple case of mistaken identity. Probably could have happened to anyone." Her voice hardened. "Thank heavens I found out the truth in time!" She whipped around, the braid flying over her shoulder to hang down the center of her back. With grim briskness, she resumed her walk in tight-lipped fury. This time, however, the fury was at her own runaway tongue. She shouldn't have tacked on that last line. It had been far too revealing and she could only hope he wouldn't pick up on it.

Court caught hold of her braid, yanking her to a violent halt before Leya had gone more than a few steps.

"Ouch!" she yelped, incensed at the small pain. "Let go of me, you sadist!"

But his response was a further, somewhat gentler tug that nevertheless managed to pull her slightly off balance and into his arms. At once, he steadied her by clamping her resisting body tightly against his broad chest.

"In time for what, Leya?" he demanded as she

wedged her hands against his shoulders. "Why are you so glad you discovered who I was by this morning?"

"No special reason," she taunted, pushing with a disgusting lack of effect against his unyielding body. The silver in her eyes glinted as she lifted a resentful gaze to meet his probing one. "It's not at all uncommon for a woman to like to know the real name of the man who took her to dinner!"

"That's not what you meant, you little shrew. Tell me the truth! Or shall I do it for you?" he offered menacingly.

"You wouldn't know how!" Leya was acutely aware of the manner in which Court's small store of patience seemed to be depleting itself. But what did she care if he lost his temper altogether? There was nothing he could do to her now!

"You're telling yourself you're glad you found out the truth because you came very close to winding up in my bed last night, and there is every possibility you would have come even closer to doing so tonight. By the end of our week here together, you would have belonged to me completely and that frightens you, doesn't it? You've realized you might have fallen for a man who made you feel like a fool."

"That's not true! You don't scare me in the least, Court Tremayne, but you do annoy the hell out of me! Kindly let me go!" Leya blazed, horrified at his perception. Her palms on his shoulders curled into fists as she struggled to escape his grasp.

"Do you think I don't know how far gone you were last night?" he snarled, disregarding her futile efforts to free herself. "I didn't have to let you go back to your own room, Leya! With very little effort, I could have kept you with me until morning and we both know it. I was the fool last night because I was trying to play the gentleman. It seemed to be what you wanted, and I, like an idiot, wanted to please you. I took a risk and let you go, and look where it's landed us!" His very male indignation would have been humorous if Leya hadn't felt equally indignant.

"How dare you act the injured party!" she nearly shrieked.

"Because I'm feeling injured!"

Before Leya fully comprehended his intent, Court had pinned her head in the crook of his arm, dragging her back against his shoulder and holding her immobile for his kiss. Even as her mouth opened in angry denial, he was crushing the resistance there with his own lips.

Leya, whose recent memories of his kisses comprised images of tantalizing, haunting, teasing caresses that urged and beckoned, was stunned by the devastating domination Court now exerted so effortlessly. Instinctively, she tried to wrench her face away from the marauding punishment, but she couldn't move so much as an inch in his grasp.

"No!" she shouted into his throat, her single word muffled in the warm heat there. Instantly, she was disciplined for her verbal rejection, Court's teeth closing painfully on her lip until she opened her teeth and allowed the invasion of his tongue. It found hers hiding in the dark cavern and forced it into a hot, savage duel that brought a moan from deep in her throat. Only when he seemed satisfied that he had subdued the defiance did he withdraw, his voice grating on her mouth.

"There's no point in fighting me, little Leya. I'm staking my claim, putting my seal of ownership on you, and you're going to learn the limits of my chain!" His hand went possessively to her breast.

The silvery green eyes flew open to glare into the molten brown ones so close to her own, Leya's flaming anger sparkling clearly. Too clearly, if she had but known it. There was far more than anger in the gems of green. There was a feverish brilliance reflecting the depth of her passionate outrage.

"You egotistical, overbearing, arrogant creature! Take your hands off me this instant! And don't have the gall to talk to me as if I were some sort of pet or slave you can own!"

He grinned with feral savagery, his fingers on her jacket splaying to cup the whole of the breast underneath. "But I am going to own you, honey. It's the only way with a woman like you. You have to be quite certain which one of us is in charge or you'll run me ragged. I'm much too lazy to let you do that to me!"

With a quick movement he obviously hadn't expected, Leya jerked one arm free and swung it. Not in the typical, useless feminine slap, but in a short-arced, forceful punch to his ribs. The thickness of his sheepskin coat blunted the impact somewhat, but there was nevertheless a satisfying thud and she heard the sharp breath between his lips.

"You little vixen!" He snagged the offending hand and crushed it in his own. "I'm going to wind up doing something we both might regret before this is over, and you'll have no one but yourself to blame!"

His head came down again, bruising her mouth. When she went taut in protest, he deliberately moved to bury his face in the curve of her throat, forcing her to accept the burning string of kisses that he trailed from the pulse to the nape of her neck. He held her tightly against his shoulder, trapping one of her arms between their bodies and holding her flailing wrist in the manacle of his grip. With his free hand, he began unzipping her down jacket.

"Court! Don't!" Leya's voice was muffled in the sheepskin. He paid her words no attention, sliding his hand smoothly under the yellow sweater and up to her breast. At the touch, her breath was suddenly blocked. When his fingers undid the front clasp of her bra and slid across to begin a rough teasing pattern on the nipple, she could only suck in air on a gasp.

"Listen to your body, not your head, sweetheart," Court ordered thickly as he held the prize of the hardened tip of her rounded breast. "God knows mine is screaming loudly enough at me! I can't believe yours isn't clamoring just as madly. We want each other, little Leya. Why shouldn't we satisfy that want?"

"There are a few things missing from this relationship, damn you!" she rasped, knowing herself helpless to continue fighting the effect he had on her for long. It enveloped her, absorbed her, seduced her sense of touch in the same way that the isolated beach did. The heat of his body was a delicious counterpoint to the crisp, chilled breeze. The earthy, tantalizing scent of him filled her nostrils like the smell of the sea, and the feel of his hands was as alluring as the sight of a storm on the waves. He could not have chosen a more overwhelming setting than the beach to make overwhelming, mastering love to her, she acknowledged miserably.

"What's missing from our relationship, Leya?" he whispered beguilingly, his hand slipping down from her curving fullness to flatten appreciatively on the skin of her stomach. He must have sensed her reaction because in another moment he was letting his fingertips trespass inside the waistband of her jeans. Leya shivered violently. Desperately, she tried to pull her wandering senses together, too conscious of the new seduction in his lips as they explored the exposed nape of her neck.

"Try love for starters!" she cried into his shoulder.

"It will come in time," he assured her in soft persuasion. "Give yourself a chance. You can fall in love with me . . ."

"I'm not particularly interested in a one-sided situation!" she hissed.

"You want me to fall in love with you?" Court gave a soft, knowing chuckle. "Even if I were to fall in love with you, I'd be a fool to admit it, wouldn't I? Especially at this point! You'd use the information like a loaded gun!"

Leya ground her teeth, hating the humor she felt in his chest. He was determined to make a joke of it!

"We'll worry about falling in love later," he went on easily, sliding his hand along the edge of the jeans until he reached the small of her back. She could feel him playing with the tiny, fine golden hairs he found there, and her body throbbed in response. "There are other matters to settle between us first," he concluded, sounding decisive.

"Love isn't the only thing I'd want out of a relationship," she swore forcefully. "There are a lot of other things you're equally incapable of giving!"

"Such as?" He put out his tongue and touched the small bones of her shoulder with its tip.

"Such as respect and equality, to name a couple!"

"Now that's an unfair accusation," he muttered. "I have every intention of teaching you to respect me. It's one of my highest priorities, in fact."

"That's not what I meant, damn you!" she wailed, wishing she could move just enough to sink her teeth into him or pummel his ribs again. But he still held her caged.

"Ah, you're afraid I don't respect you!"

"It's quite obvious you don't!"

"You're wrong, Leya. I have a very healthy respect for your strength and your intelligence and your independence. The same sort of respect I have for a female lion. But a man has to tame wild things somewhat if he intends to enjoy them in some measure of safety. I wanted to try a gentling approach first. That's why you got off so easily last night. But if that doesn't work . . ."

"I'm surprised you are willing to devote the energy it would take to control me," Leya ground out bitterly. "I got the impression you enjoyed a leisurely approach to life!"

"I do. It's one of the things we have in common," he grinned and she felt his teeth on her skin. "Don't worry. This little flare-up between us is a temporary thing. Once the dust has settled, we'll both be able to lapse happily back into our normal, serene lifestyles." He sounded pleased at the prospect.

Leya froze in sudden anguish. My God! she thought helplessly, he sees me as some sort of temporary toy to relieve a small stretch of boredom he's passing through!

It was either that or he was convinced she would undermine his influence with Keith. Those were the only two reasons Leya's agile mind could come up with for Court's apparent interest in her as a lover. She had been an idiot during the past two days to think he was genuinely attracted to her!

And how typical of a man to think that the best way of controlling a woman, whether for one's own pleasure or for business reasons, was to take her to bed!

Chapter Four

If you've quite finished with the explanation you brought me down here for, do you mind letting me go back to the inn?" Leya managed to mumble into Court's shoulder.

She felt his alert silence and then he said carefully, "That depends. Are you going to accept the explanation?"

"You actually want me to forgive you for your deceit?" she muttered disbelievingly.

"I want you to understand why I did it and let us both start over again. Hell, Leya," he went on wryly, "I know we've gotten off on the wrong foot because of that contract. . . ."

"Your perception is blinding!" she interrupted scathingly.

"But I'm asking you to forget it and let us start fresh," he persisted doggedly. "I want you so much, little Leya, and I know the feeling is mutual. You can't hide it from me. In the past couple of days, we've gotten too close."

"And if I don't agree to forgive and forget?"

He sighed deep in his chest. "Then we'll do things the hard way."

"Meaning?" she gritted, as his hand slid out from under the sweater. The loss of its warmth was unexpectedly depressing, and she could have kicked herself for the irrational reaction.

"Honey, don't push me," he replied steadily. "Just give me a chance. Please?" Slowly, he loosened his grip, not setting her completely free, but allowing some distance between them.

Leya watched him through resentful eyes, disgusted to find a tiny spark of humor flicker to life at the effort he was making to appear encouragingly repentant.

"You don't grovel very well," she noted grimly.

"Is that what you want me to do?" he rapped interestedly, tortoiseshell eyes flickering with an unreadable expression.

"It would be a start, but don't fret," she added quickly, flinging up a hand. "I don't expect it of you!"

"Leya, from now on I guarantee that everything between us will be honest and straightforward," he replied earnestly. His large hands moved to zip up the down jacket.

"Or else they'll be sneaky and underhanded. One of the two, right?" she retorted cheekily, rapidly regaining her nerve as she recognized that his impassioned anger of a few moments earlier was fading.

"I'm trying to be patient . . ." he began forcefully.

"Why? Because you're hoping I'll give in to your

blandishments and therefore be much less taxing to handle?''

The hint of a smile touched his mouth. "I'll have to admit life would be simpler if you decided to be reasonable.''

"Oh! You're impossible!" Disgustedly, Leya thrust her hands into her pockets and stalked back up the beach toward the distant inn. She didn't look up as he fell into step beside her, but she heard the questioning note in his voice.

"Leya?" He was waiting for her ultimate answer, she realized, asking if she was going to make things difficult for him.

And it struck her that Court was still wary of her. True, he had her signature on the contract, but she retained half-ownership of the firm. As long as she held fifty percent of the shares, she could still represent a threat to his control. He himself had pointed out that all she would need to do was convince Keith they'd made a mistake . . .

Something inside her despaired. She didn't want to think Court was really so unscrupulous. She didn't want to acknowledge the possibility that he was still scheming. With a small inner sigh, she realized why. She was attracted to the man. Attracted to him in a way she had never been attracted to anyone else. She simply didn't want to believe the worst of him. In spite of the evidence!

But she had to be realistic, she told herself fiercely. The only thing she could be sure of was that Court wasn't completely confident of her. He was prepared to exert himself if she proved rebellious. He was equally prepared to accept her surrender immediately. But what would he do, she wondered acidly, if she didn't give him the clearcut answer he wanted? It was a poor punishment for the humiliation he had put her through, but it was all she had.

"I'll have to think about it," she told him coolly.

"Think about it!" he exploded. "What do you mean, think about it? Either you're going to accept the situation or you aren't!"

"Whatever you say, Court," she replied demurely, trying to take some satisfaction from his obvious frustration. It was hard. She didn't want the satisfaction of punishing him. She wanted the satisfaction of knowing he really wanted her!

"What do you think you're playing at, Leya Brandon?" he growled. "You were ready to commit murder when you opened the door this morning. A few minutes ago you were shivering in my arms. Make up your mind, damn it!"

"I'll try," she promised mockingly. "But first I think I'll have breakfast. There's nothing like a brisk morning walk on the beach to stir up an appetite, don't you agree?"

She watched him out of the corner of her slanting green eyes and saw the look of wariness and confusion tautening his features.

"Then what?" he prodded belligerently.

"After breakfast? Why, then I think I'll make arrangements to head back to Santa Rosa, of course. I'm sure you'll understand when I say my vacation has been spoiled!"

"There's no need to turn tail and run." He had apparently reached the conclusion that she was afraid of him.

"I'm not running," she assured him with forced serenity, "I'm flying. There's a plane out of that little town up the coast that connects with a major airline. I'll be home by noon."

There was a heavy silence.

"I drove up," Court said finally. "I'll drive you back."

Leya was startled. "No thanks," she managed. "It's a full day's trip by car and I don't think I want to be cooped up with you for that long."

"Leya!"

"Yes, Court?" she said with vast, insincere politeness.

"I said I'll drive you if you're determined to go back to Santa Rosa today!"

She sensed his uncertainty and impatience and wondered at it. A part of her longed to believe it stemmed from the fact that he was finding his victory hollow. But she knew better than that. The only reason Court was making an effort to maintain some relationship with her was because he was nervous about the power she still held over him. True, Keith practically idolized the older man now, but if his determined sister went to work on him, who was to say she might not be able to convince her brother they'd made a mistake? She still held a fifty-percent ownership in Brandon Security.

But the thought of spending several more hours with Court was suddenly too tempting. Leya was honest enough to admit to herself that she was looking for excuses to put off a final break in their relationship. She didn't want to say good-bye. Regardless of his reasoning, Court was offering her an excuse to stay close to him for a few more hours. And Leya, fearing she was a fool, found herself grasping at the straw.

"All right, Court."

In the end, the trip back to Northern California proved to be the battleground of a very delicate, very careful war. Leya realized within the first hour that Court was determined to use the time to his advantage.

He knows he hasn't handled this well, she found herself thinking in surprise. He's realized he needs more than my signature. He needs my cooperation. She realized a little grimly that he was going to try and ensure that cooperation by trading on the attraction between them. What frightened her was the possibility he might succeed in doing exactly that! She remembered their lovemaking the previous evening and on the beach that morning and shivered. She had never known such depths of passion with any other man. It was unique. Court Tremayne was unique. And telling herself she was a unique idiot didn't seem to do much good.

There were no outright confrontations. Court was obviously going out of his way to try and mend the fences he'd ripped apart. Leya caught his deceptively casual glances from time to time as he drove with an assurance that seemed second nature.

Leya was careful to steer the conversation in relatively harmless directions, but Court was equally bent on making his case. The subtle battle raged back and forth.

"Honey," he began determinedly at one point, "when you've had a chance to think about it, you're going to remember how much we were enjoying each other during the two days we just spent together. We learned a lot during that time and . . ."

"Just look at those fantastic redwoods!" Leya interrupted in an awestruck tone. "Do you realize how old these trees are? The whole forest seems so . . . so primeval, doesn't it? A piece of the earth lost in time." As the magnificent coastal redwoods drifted past the car window, Leya focused her attention entirely upon them.

"I've lined up an apartment in Santa Rosa," Court tried again later. "I want you to see it . . ."

"Oh, darn," Leya muttered, her fingers going to one ear. "I've lost an earring. It must have fallen on the beach this morning and I just now noticed it."

She heard Court stifle a groan of dissatisfaction at her refusal to get involved in an intimate discussion. "Was it expensive?" he muttered.

"Well, yes, considering the time I put into it," Leya grumbled. That was no less than the truth, she thought. She really ought to go ahead and get her ears pierced.

That succeeded in surprising him. "Time?" he asked with sudden interest, casting her an appraising glance. "Do you make jewelry?"

She nodded.

"Including that green thing you were wearing last night? I liked that. It was very unusual." He sounded genuinely admiring.

"I make all my own jewelry." She shrugged, a little sorry she had brought up the topic by noticing her missing earring.

"No kidding? You have a little workshop?"

"Well, yes," she returned distantly.

"Do you sell your stuff?"

"Oh, no. I only make things for myself or for friends. Just a hobby."

"I'm surprised you don't have your ears pierced," he remarked knowledgeably. "I've heard women say it's a safer way to wear good earrings."

"I'm a born coward," Leya confessed, smiling slightly in spite of herself.

"Is that the reason you haven't done it?" He grinned. "You amaze me. I wouldn't have thought you would be afraid of a little thing like that!" He seemed, she thought in annoyance, delighted at the news of this fault in her character!

"I don't see many men rushing out to do themselves a physical injury for the sake of fashion!"

He laughed. "I'm sure everyone, male and female, makes some sort of painful effort in the never-ending chore of trying to attract the opposite sex! I've got friends who jog for miles and then lift weights. Painful in the extreme, I should think!"

"And what sort of painful effort do you put forth, Court?" Leya demanded, eager to put him at least vaguely on the defensive.

"My effort is that of acting with a semblance of civilized behavior when what I really want to do is reach out and drag you straight into bed," he retorted immediately, eyes darkening with a sudden intensity that was unnerving.

Leya felt the blood rush into her face. She had walked right into that one.

They stopped for dinner early in the evening, and it

was dark before Court, following Leya's terse directions, finally drew his very sleek foreign car to a halt in the quiet neighborhood.

For a moment, he sat in silence surveying the old two-story structure with its encircling porch, graceful windows, and gingerbread trim. The new wooden siding was painted a rich butterscotch and the trim was in white. Her home dated from a warmer, more inviting era of house design, and Leya had taken loving care of it in the two years she had owned it.

"You live here?" Court's voice held something besides admiration, and Leya's head swung around sharply. What could he possibly find to criticize about her beautiful home?

"Yes," she told him tartly.

"Alone? In a big place like this?" His considering, dangerous glance told its own tale.

"It's a bit late to be worrying about who I might be living with, isn't it?" she taunted.

"It's a bit late for you to be telling me about it," he corrected in a hard, raw voice that alarmed her. "But better late than never, I suppose. Let's get it over." He shoved open the car door with a savage push.

Leya saw the thin, brutal line of his mouth, the uncompromising set of his shoulders, and realized she was looking at a man who had psyched himself into a battle-ready frame of mind in about five seconds flat.

"Court!" she yelped belatedly, realizing what she'd done. Hastily, she scrambled out of her side of the car and raced forward to catch his arm.

"Court, there's no one in there," she said breathlessly, tugging at his sleeve. "Stop acting the demented lover! The neighbors might see you!"

"If he's not there, where is he?" Court ripped out, shooting her a look of smoldering rage. "When does he get home at night? Or have you two got some sort of *modern* relationship? One that lets you go off on vacation while he does the town? I warn you, it's not going to be like that between us!"

Leya swallowed, realizing with inner disgust that it was going to be harder calming Court back into a rational state than it had been getting him out of it in the first place. Was he really this upset at the thought of her living with a man? Was his interest in her more than merely business? She didn't have time to dwell on the possibility now.

"Don't be ridiculous," she ordered disdainfully. "I'm not sharing that house with anyone. It's all mine! But it certainly wouldn't be your concern if I did have a male roommate," she went on spiritedly, her eyes glittering. "What in the world did you think you were going to accomplish by barging into my home like that, even if there had been someone there?"

"That's obvious! I'd have thrown him out!" The adrenaline in him was fading, but the expression in the molten eyes remained hard.

"You'd have had absolutely no right! I've given you no excuse to think . . ."

"Are we going to stand on your front porch and discuss what has turned out to be a purely hypothetical point?" he asked with sudden rough humor, his hand grasping the long dark braid on her shoulder and tugging affectionately.

"Yes, we most certainly are! We're going to get something very clear between us, Court Tremayne! I will not have you embarrassing me in front of friends and neighbors . . ."

"Never," he promised solemnly. "Wouldn't think of it!" The outrageously pious expression on his face made her want to hit him.

"Nor will I have you making scenes with any of my *male* friends," she emphasized.

"How many of them are there?" he demanded interestedly.

"Will you be serious?"

"Anything you say. I am hereby seriously asking you out to dinner tomorrow night," he said at once. "Seven o'clock okay?"

"I haven't even said I'll go out with you!" she blazed, thoroughly irritated now.

"You didn't give me all this trouble during our two days at the beach," he complained on a note of smothered laughter. "Can't you close your eyes and imagine yourself back there, B.C.?"

"B.C.?" she questioned warily.

"Before Contract."

"You're an idiot," she sighed.

"But a lovable one," he argued, bending his head to drop a feathery kiss on her nose. "Besides, it takes one to know one. Come on and I'll get your bags out of the car."

Twenty minutes later, Leya watched from her screen door as the sleek black car pulled away from the curb and thought herself extremely lucky to have rid herself of Courtland Gannon Tremayne so easily. It could have gotten nasty, she reflected uncomfortably as she turned away and locked the door behind her. Fortunately, he had convinced himself that she would be dutifully waiting at seven o'clock tomorrow night to go out to dinner with him and that seemed to satisfy him. His good-bye kiss had been short and fierce.

And what would happen, she wondered with grim interest, when he arrived and found her gone? Because she certainly didn't intend to go out with him the following evening. She needed time to think.

Automatically, she dialed her brother's number to let him know she was back in town.

"I thought you were going to stay for a few more days," Keith responded a moment later, sounding vastly surprised. "What happened? Weather turn too bad? A volcano erupt?"

That last guess wasn't far from the truth, Leya reflected wryly. It occurred to her she wasn't sure yet how much she wanted to tell Keith. Her pride was at stake here. Did she really want to admit to him what a fool she had been? And then there was the fact that Keith sounded so happy to know she'd signed the contract. Did she really want to ruin his working relationship with Court before the partnership had had a fair chance? What if Court turned out to be the salvation of Brandon Security after all?

"After I'd made up my mind about the contract, I saw no reason to hang around," she told him evasively, not wanting to acknowledge the fact that she was making excuses to herself. Why was it so difficult to take a hard stand against Court Tremayne? Why was she trying to find a reason to give him a chance?

"Court was a little upset when you failed to show up for the meeting he'd planned," Keith went on with a chuckle. "I was a bit worried that he might rile you when he finally found you but I gather everything went okay. He's a great guy when you get to know him," he assured her enthusiastically. "I'm going to learn a lot from him."

Leya couldn't think of an intelligent response to that comment, so she mumbled something noncommittal and largely inaudible.

"Say, as long as you're back early," her brother continued, "you might want to drop by Sue's tomorrow evening. She's giving a cocktail party and said to be sure and extend the invitation to you if you got back into town in time." Susan Adams was a mutual friend of long standing.

Leya didn't hesitate. It was the perfect answer. Now she had an excuse not to be at home for Court tomorrow night! "I'd love to. Thanks for telling me. What time?"

"Six-thirty or so. It's a buffet, so we won't starve," he told her cheerfully. "I'll see you there. And Leya?"

"Yes, Keith?"

"Thanks for signing that contract." The phone clattered into the cradle.

For a long time, Leya sat silently beside the phone, gazing with unseeing eyes out over the cheery clutter of her living room. The inside of her home, as friendly as the outside, reflected its owner's lack of concern for unnecessary order. Leya's financial accounts for her bookshop were accurate to the penny, but the interior of her home was warm and delightfully chaotic. The difference represented an essential aspect of her character, and she was far too intelligent not to be aware of it. She had long since accepted her leisurely approach to life, seeing no point in overexerting herself in nonessential areas. The house was clean, but on its best days it remained—at least to an impartial observer— mildly disorganized. That didn't bother Leya in the slightest. She knew herself to be smart enough to set her own priorities in life, and perfect housekeeping simply wasn't one of them.

But where, she asked herself thoughtfully as she viewed her highly eclectic décor, did Courtland Gannon Tremayne fit into her list of priorities? She shook her head, her eyes roving idly over the excellent nineteenth-century end tables and the twentieth-century batik wall hangings. Why was she tacitly admitting to herself that, even though she had every reason to mistrust him, her instinctive reaction to Court was to believe he would honorably uphold his end of the contract? Her teeth clenched for an instant. When she thought of how close she had come to letting him seduce her!

There was no doubt about it, she acknowledged sadly, her pride had been the chief casualty in their small war. It had been a long time since a man had so completely played her for a fool. She closed her lashes against the memory of Court's kisses and her own mindless response.

But it wasn't only the passion she remembered, it was the humor they had shared and the conversation and the walks on the beach. It all added up to a very dangerous package, and if she had half the brains she credited herself with, she would tell Keith everything and demand they unite to fire the man!

Well, she decided as she slowly got to her feet and made her way into the cozy bedroom with its huge brass bed, she would have a small breather in which to think about what she wanted to do.

Leya was still running through her reactions to Court the next afternoon as she turned off the shower and reached for one of the huge, brilliant red towels that decorated the cheerful red-and-white bathroom. Most of the day, she had been unable to think of much else besides the man, and the fact annoyed her. Perhaps the party this evening would take her mind off the puzzle he presented.

The towel wrapped around her torso and tucked in just above her breast, she pulled a brush through the unbound deep-brown hair until it fell in a rich mass down her back. She would rebraid it when she had dressed. Maybe she would twine through her hair the beaded metal ribbon she had completed last week, she thought, opening the door of the warm, steamy bath and stepping into her bedroom.

A scream rose in her throat even as she recognized the large male figure standing by the window. She barely stifled it, her hand going to her mouth in classic shock. Immediate fear was replaced at once by unadulterated outrage.

"Court! What the hell do you think you're doing in my bedroom! How dare you?" She clutched automatically at the fastening of the towel but her mind was churning with too much anger to be overly cautious at that point.

He turned, gold-misted eyes sweeping the length of her figure encased only in the towel and coming to rest on the flaming silver-green gaze. Something stirred in his expression. Something primitive and masculine and dangerous. But he smiled. And that smile made Leya more wary than anything else he might have done.

"I came to take you to the party," he said simply, not moving.

"The party," she repeated stupidly. "But . . ."

"I know we had a date for dinner, but I'm agreeable to a change of plans. Fortunately, your brother filled me in on the change, though. Otherwise there might have been a most unfortunate misunderstanding between us." Still he didn't move, watching her with his hands clasped casually behind his back. Leya had the impression he did that to keep from reaching for her throat.

"I never said I would go out with you this evening," she started aggressively. Going on the offense was the only thing she could think to do under the circumstances. Perhaps she could bluff him.

"You allowed me to believe you were accepting my invitation and you know it," he returned coolly.

"You assume far too much!"

"Because I want you so much," he countered. "Although at the moment I might find it more satisfying to beat you than make love to you!"

"How did you get in here?" she shot back suspiciously, her mouth hardening with hostility. "The front door was locked. I know it was locked!"

"Ah, but not with a Brandon Security Systems lock," he murmured. "You really should use the family brand, Leya. It's very good, and living alone in a big house like this you should take every precaution!"

"This is the first time in two years I've had any reason to worry!"

"Are you worried, little Leya? If so, then I commend your intelligence."

"Are you resorting to threats, Court?" she demanded boldly.

"I told you once I prefer the easiest, least taxing methods."

"Get out of here!" she hissed violently.

He moved abruptly, starting toward her with long, lean strides that ate up the distance between them before she could get back into the bathroom and lock the door. Her hand was on the knob behind her when his fingers closed on her bare shoulder.

He jerked her toward him, bringing her close against his long-sleeved yellow shirt and dark brown slacks. He wasn't wearing a necktie, and the open collar revealed the tanned line of his throat and the beginnings of crisp, curling chest hair.

"Stop it!" Leya clutched frantically at the towel's insecure fastening, which was threatening to come undone under the violent treatment it was receiving.

He grasped both of her wrists and pulled them around behind his back, forcing her head to tip up and her eyes to meet his.

"The only way you're going to keep that towel in place," he pointed out with drawling amusement, "is to stand very close to me. The fact that it's still between us is your best hope right now."

"Take your hands off me," she snarled, knowing herself physically helpless and hating the sensation. "You're behaving like a . . . a . . ." Words failed her.

"Like something besides a gentleman?" he suggested almost mildly, eyes gleaming as he forced her close. "But you have only yourself to blame for that, don't you? A *lady* who makes plans to break a date shouldn't expect too chivalrous a response from the man involved!"

"I've told you, I never agreed to go out with you tonight! You ordered me to do so, but for your information, that is not considered the same as an invitation!"

"Details," he growled softly, lowering his head to touch her forehead and then her cheekbones with his lips. "But I'm willing to let bygones be bygones. Unlike some people I know! Show me you're sorry and I'll show you how lenient I can be. Come on, Leya, a pretty little apology," he coaxed with mocking charm as he feathered her face with more and more warm, tiny kisses. Kisses that beguiled and cajoled just as they had that night she had almost wound up in his bed, Leya reminded herself fiercely, as she tried to retain her basic good sense.

"Court, you've had your big scene," she muttered, aware of the heat in her body and terribly afraid he must know of it also. She had so little on that she was literally unable to clothe her reactions. "Please get out of here and let me get dressed!"

"But I like you wearing only a towel," he whispered deeply, his teeth nibbling at her ear and the sensitive area behind it. "You seem much less formidable this way, do you know that? And the softness of your hair is an invitation to any man, especially one who happens to be in your bedroom."

"Please!" she almost begged, acutely aware of her body's rising tide of response. How could she let this—this *liar* take advantage of her? What was wrong with her? But she had been thinking of him all day, and it was as if his sudden and totally unexpected presence in her room was the result of her overactive imagination. As if she had somehow conjured him up out of thin air from the sheer force of her thoughts!

She heard his muffled groan and knew his own body was leaping into hard, demanding alertness. It called to her on a nonverbal level, seeking her, wanting to bury itself in her warmth. The gentle, teasing quality of the kisses changed gradually, deepening into the heavy, drugging, seductive caresses that had left her so helpless on the beach the previous morning.

"You can't hide from me, honey," he grated, his mouth sliding moistly, burningly along her cheek to cover her lips in a plundering, arousing kiss that shook off the last of the gentle cajolery and bared the uncompromising male desire beneath.

"I know you want me. It's only your silly female pride standing in the way," he murmured against her bruised lips. "But I've apologized for that business with the contract. Forgive me for that and I'll forgive you for trying to sneak out tonight!"

"It's not that simple, damn you," she wailed, her lashes moving restlessly against her cheeks as she felt the throbbing in her stomach.

"Yes, it is," he countered throatily. "It's as simple as getting rid of the towel between us!" With that he moved against her, his chest crushing her breasts for an instant before he stepped back a couple of inches.

The red towel gave up the battle and slipped soundlessly to the floor at their feet.

"No!" Leya whimpered, and then her words were swallowed up as he forced his tongue deeply into her mouth and his arms released hers to encircle her still-damp, nude body.

It was getting worse, she thought frantically while she could still think at all. Every time he held her she was less able to resist, less able to deny him. She felt the firm thrust of his strong thighs as he lowered his hands the length of her back and arched her hips into him. His fingers snarled themselves in the long ends of her hair and used the leverage to force her head back further so that his mouth could explore her throat.

"God, Leya!" he swore, his lips branding her, "I love the feel of you. I could get lost in your body. So much passion waiting for me, so much pleasure. I've wanted you since I first saw you across the lobby at that inn! You're going to drive me crazy if you don't admit you want me, too!"

"But that's not enough!" she gasped as his fingers dug into the soft flesh of her buttocks. A violent shiver rocked her.

"It's a damn good start!" he retorted, using his grip to force her into full awareness of his growing desire.

The unmistakable desire in him was a commanding, aggressive pull on the very core of her femininity. It stirred her loins and weakened her knees until she was clinging to him for support.

"Yes," he whispered in thick triumph as he felt her clasping hands move over his back. It was as if he were accepting a surrender she hadn't voiced aloud, and it shook her back to awareness as nothing else could have done in that moment.

"Let go of me, Court!" she ordered in a rough, shaking voice. "We're going to a party, not to bed!"

She struggled wildly, as much against the masculine triumph she perceived in him as against the force of her own desire. He was not going to make a complete fool out of her!

"Sweetheart, don't fight us both. You can't possibly win," he purred huskily in her ear, his hands gentling her spine. "It's going to be all right. Let me show you how good it's going to be between us. You can trust me . . ."

"About as far as I can throw you!" With a last, desperate push, Leya wrenched herself free and grabbed madly for the towel. She clutched it tight around her trembling body and backed slowly away from him. He followed her with his eyes but made no move to recapture his victim.

"You've got a lot of nerve telling me to trust you after what you did to me!" she blazed, sweeping one hand harshly through her disarrayed hair. "And now you've come sneaking into my house like a common thief!"

"You'd better hurry if we're to get there on time," he interrupted absently, glancing at the thin gold watch on his browned wrist.

"What?" she managed, taken aback. She eyed him in confusion. "If you think I'm really going to that party with you . . ."

"You just said you were," he reminded her with deceptive casualness. A casualness that didn't hide the underlying steel. "You said we were going to a party and not to bed. You wouldn't think of backing out of a second date with me, now would you?"

"Court—!" Leya began wrathfully, a growing conviction that she was being manipulated eating into her bones.

"Get dressed, Leya, or I'll help you," he ordered calmly.

"The only thing you'll do is get out of my bedroom! Now!"

"Darling," he murmured in a tone of weary patience, "I'm trying very hard to tame my shrew with kindness and a degree of gentleness but if she doesn't learn the limits of how far she can push me that way, I'll be forced to try another technique. The choice is up to her. Which is it to be?"

"You're insufferable!"

"You're intoxicating. Even when you're scowling at me," he retorted smoothly. "Fifteen minutes? I'll wait for you downstairs."

Leya stared at his broad back as he sauntered out of the room. Never in her entire life had a man ever told her she was intoxicating.

She deliberately stretched the fifteen minutes to twenty but didn't quite have the nerve to push it any farther. It wasn't that she was the least bit afraid of Court Tremayne, Leya reassured herself, it was just that he was a great deal larger than she was and he was currently blocking the only exits out of the house. And she had been intending to go to the party anyway.

With any luck, she told herself in renewed spirit as she descended the stairs a few minutes past the deadline, she would find some opportunity at the party to repay Court for his ill-treatment. At the very least, she would make certain she had another ride home. Keith would be there and he could be relied upon to provide transportation. Court Tremayne might be escorting her to the event but she didn't intend to allow him to bring her home!

The subject of her thoughts lifted his streaked brown head as she came toward him, tossing aside a magazine on gemstones as he got to his feet. He was smiling with that curious, proprietary smile of a man who thinks he has only to put out his hand and the prize will be his.

"More of your own hand-crafted jewelry?" he asked, his eyes going to the unusual chains at her neck, which nestled in the hollow of a high-standing oriental collar. The dress was a boldly marked sheath of red and gold.

She nodded curtly, stepping lightly aside to collect her shawl as his fingers reached out to touch the necklace. The small evasion served its purpose, but when she glanced at him again she could have sworn she surprised a strange degree of hurt in the tortoise-shell eyes. It was gone in an instant as his hand dropped to his side.

"You can't avoid it forever, you know," he cautioned softly as he took her arm and started toward the door. He slanted a glance down at her profile, his eyes lingering on the dark braid. "Sooner or later you'll have to forgive me. Why not make it now? Tonight?"

"Think how much easier that would be for you," she scoffed sweetly. "No need to exert yourself at all!"

He grinned wryly. "I knew you'd understand."

"Sorry, Court, you're not getting off that easily," she muttered waspishly.

"What are your terms?" he demanded cheerfully, opening the car door for her.

"I'm still drafting them."

"Let's hope I don't entirely run out of patience

before you decide how I'm supposed to make up for my misdeeds," he observed politely.

It was only as she walked into the party on his arm that Leya finally found something to take her mind temporarily off the matter of her entanglement with Court Tremayne.

She would have preferred almost any other diversion. Across the room, she met the sophisticated and cynical blue eyes of the one other man in her life who had succeeded in making a fool of Leya Brandon.

Alex Harlow lifted his glass in the faintest of salutes.

Chapter Five

$\mathcal{W}$ho is he?"

Ten minutes into the flurry of welcome and introductions, Court managed to growl the question into Leya's ear. Any hope that he hadn't sensed her almost imperceptible stiffening as they had come through the door died.

"Who?" she tried, stalling uncertainly for time, although she wasn't quite sure why. The drink in her hand was cold, and Court was standing so close she could feel the heat of him. The two sensations seemed to feed her fever-pitched light-headedness. Once again, she wished desperately she wasn't so susceptible to the tactile quality of life.

He scolded her with his glance. "That guy with the light brown hair on the other side of the room, wearing a black turtleneck. You can't miss him, Leya," he added derisively. "He's the one trying to eat you alive with his eyes. The one person you haven't smiled at yet. Who the hell is he?"

"Why do you care?" she countered, sipping at her drink and smiling over the rim of the glass at their hostess. Sleek, charming, and blonde, Susan Adams had made no secret of her fascination with Court from the moment she had greeted him. She was still flicking speculative glances his way as she circulated among her guests.

"It's always nice to know the name of the guy you might have to pound to a pulp later!"

Leya flinched in astonishment, covering the reaction quickly with a less than humorous smile. "I can certainly understand your interest in getting a person's correct name. I've got some strong feelings on the matter myself!"

"Leya!" he snapped out, and she knew he had just run dry of patience. He took a sip of the scotch in his glass and waited, golden eyes pinning her. The tension in him was a lazy, coiled cat waiting to leap.

Leya quickly decided the best approach was to brazen out the situation.

"You wouldn't want to pound him, Court. You'll probably like the man. The two of you have a great deal in common!" The flashing silver in her green eyes hardened, and cool mockery edged her curving lips.

"What's that supposed to mean?" There was unmistakable anger in him now.

"A year ago I was on the point of considering marriage to him," Leya said carelessly, taking another sip from her drink. What did she care if Court knew the truth? He knew so much about her already, she thought grimly. "I thought we were in love, you see," she added confidingly, her tones laced with heavy self-mockery.

"And?" he prompted harshly through set teeth.

"And—" Leya snapped her fingers with assumed nonchalance. "Presto! He made a fool of me." The silver in her eyes gave them a dangerous gleam.

"How?" Court grated. "Don't make me drag it out of you sentence by sentence, damn it!"

Her eyes widened. "I don't see why I should let you drag it out of me at all."

"Because whatever happened is still affecting you. You look as tense and brittle as glass. I can't figure out if you want to go over to him and throw yourself into his arms or strangle him!"

"Does it matter?" she purred, not quite looking at him but aware of his braced tension as if it were a palpable thing. It made her feel even more keyed up.

"It matters! And stop drinking that stuff as if it were soda pop," he ordered in a short-tempered rasp.

"My, you are in a domineering mood this evening," she noted with biting amusement. Deliberately, she took another sip.

"I'm in a mood to whale the daylights out of you, Leya, so you might want to exercise a bit of caution."

"I was wrong back in Oregon when I accused you of having a one-track mind," she murmured smoothly, beginning to enjoy herself for some unknown reason. "I'll have to admit you've got at least two tracks when it comes to dealing with women: sex and brutality. Have you had a lot of luck with the combined approach in the past?"

"I've never had to try combining them," he drawled in a deadly cool tone. "But for you I'll make an exception. Tell me who he is, Leya, or I'll start with the brutality first."

"My brother will break your neck!"

"Your brother hasn't even arrived yet. Besides, he's got enough sense to stay out of a situation like this!"

Leya considered him, her neat head tipped to one side, her eyes bright and daring. "His name is Alex Harlow. Want to meet him?"

"Not particularly." Court faced her coolly. "Finish the story."

"There's not much to tell." She shrugged. "He used me as a cover for his relationship with a friend of mine. A married friend. I discovered what was going on the day she announced her divorce to marry Alex. End of story."

"Not quite," he disagreed dryly. "Did he wind up marrying your presumably ex-friend?"

"Oh, yes. As soon as her divorce was final. I'm sure you'll understand when I tell you I haven't seen much of either of them socially since!"

"Is his wife here tonight?"

"I haven't seen her," Leya muttered, downing another swallow of her drink.

"Then"—Court put out a hand and forcibly removed her glass—"putting the facts together we are forced to the conclusion that he's on the make this evening. You're not to get near him, is that clear?" The brown-and-gold eyes confronted her with absolute command.

Leya lifted one eyebrow in response. "Jealous, Court?" she teased. "Or just worried that you don't have as much control as you would like over the 'silent partner' in Brandon Security?" The challenge hung in the air between them, goading and provoking.

He set her half-empty glass down on the table behind him and straightened slowly, his eyes never leaving hers. "Would you like me to admit to the jealousy, little Leya?" he drawled.

"Yes," she retorted unhesitatingly, lips curved in near-laughter. "Yes, I think that might be fun!"

"I have to assume from that statement that you've never felt the full weight of a man's jealousy," he stated very softly.

Leya pretended to consider that and then shook her head decisively. "No, I can think of a few occasions when I've been privileged to witness what's been labeled jealousy. Frankly, it appeared to be a rather crude form of pouting. Like little boys who don't get their own way and go off in a corner to sulk. Would you sulk if I went over and spoke to Alex?" she asked with a strange brightness.

"No, Leya, I won't sulk," he said in a hard voice.

"Ah, well." She pretended to sigh. "It was only an outside chance. Still, it might have been fun."

"You're wrong on that point." Court looked as if he were going to pursue the subject and then broke off, glancing over her shoulder. "There's your brother. He just walked in the door."

Leya didn't look around. "A gorgeous blonde on his arm?"

"Well, she's definitely blonde. I guess you could say she's gorgeous, that is if one didn't mind a certain lack of intelligence around the eyes. Why?" Court glanced down at her wry expression.

"Since when has a man minded a certain lack of intelligence in his dates? Could I have my drink back, please?" she added with undue politeness, green eyes on the glass behind him.

"No. You've had enough."

"I haven't even finished my first drink, for heaven's sake!" she muttered furiously.

"Maybe in a little while you can have another. Provided you don't down it like water."

"You certainly are out to ruin my evening, aren't you?" she groaned.

"Chalk it up to my naturally perverse nature. You never answered my question about the blonde your brother came in with. Don't you like her?"

Leya did bother to glance around briefly at the question, her green eyes moving swiftly over the lovely young woman standing beside her good-looking, dark-headed brother.

"Never saw her before in my life," she admitted freely. "So I really can't say if I'll like her or not."

"How did you know she was blonde?" Court demanded curiously.

"That's all my brother's been dating for the past year. Blondes. Beautiful and, for the most part, empty-headed blondes." Leya frowned, slanting Court an upward glance. "Are you going to encourage or discourage that tendency in him during the next two years?"

"Your brother's contracting with me to teach him about business, not about women," Court murmured politely. "There's not much I could do about it, anyway. It's a taste a man either outgrows or he doesn't."

"Really? And have you outgrown your taste for gorgeous blondes?" Leya tossed back with an ease she didn't feel. Susan Adams was still sending interested glances in Court's direction.

"Yes, in point of fact I have," he growled, meeting her eyes very directly.

"How long did the taste persist before you saw the light?" she taunted.

"Until quite recently," he confessed airily.

"You mean my brother could go on another ten years dating those creatures?"

"Unless he gets lucky before that." Court grinned suddenly. "And finds himself a wasp-tongued shrew with hair the color of a jungle cat. Don't begrudge him the blondes in the meantime, though. They're the ones who will make him appreciate the shrew when he finds her! Come on," he went on firmly, taking her arm, "we'd better go over and say hello. Keith's seen us."

Effortlessly, Court pushed a way through the crowd toward the other couple, dragging Leya along in his wake like a toy. She did manage to snag a glass from a passing tray, however, and had it secured in the hand farthest away from her escort by the time they reached Keith and his blonde. Her brother's green eyes met hers as she approached on Court's arm. His eyes lacked the silver tinge of her own, but the dark brown of his hair was similar. And the basic underlying intelligence, she had always thought, was pure Brandon. That opinion remained in place in spite of his recent decision to sign the contract with Court Tremayne.

"Hi, Leya," Keith greeted her affectionately. "Glad you could make it tonight. Sorry you cut your vacation short, though. Good evening, Court, taking good care of my sister?" The vivid green of his eyes absorbed the protective way Leya's arm was tucked under Court's and the abnormal brightness in his sister's eyes.

"You can trust me to look after her," Court said easily, smiling at the blonde. "Who are you in charge of tonight?"

"This is Angie," Keith grinned cheerfully. Angie didn't appear to be blessed with a last name but she didn't seem to mind as the introductions were made. Her beautifully made-up blue eyes were full of a sultry invitation and the sexy red pout of her mouth was glistening with too much lip gloss.

"I'm glad to see you and Court hitting it off so well, Leya," Keith remarked with a poorly concealed smile.

"Did you have a few doubts?" Leya charged sweetly, lifting her glass for a swallow.

"Where the hell did you get that?" Court interrupted before her brother could respond. He reached for the glass, but Leya managed to neatly sidestep.

"If you'll excuse me, I think I'll find the ladies' room. Don't go away, Court, I'll be right back!" With a quick turn on her heel that swirled the red-and-gold skirt around her ankles, Leya swept off into the crowd, glass clutched tightly in her hand. She could feel Court's eyes on her for a moment but knew he wasn't following. When the prickling sensation at the back of her neck ceased, she veered from the direction in which she had been going and headed for the terrace instead.

There was no one else outside to share the cold night air and the view of Santa Rosa's lights, so Leya sipped her drink in peace, her arms folded against the chill. And she thought about the same thing she had been thinking about all day: Court Tremayne. The only break came when her mind went briefly, angrily to the presence of Alex Harlow. But upset as she was at seeing Alex's cynical, handsome face again, there was no denying that Court somehow loomed the larger of the two in her mind tonight.

"Hello, Leya." Alex's voice came from the shadows behind her. Well, hadn't she been half-expecting it? Wasn't that the real reason she'd come out here alone for a few minutes? To see if he'd follow? She knew what that look in his eyes had meant when she'd first seen it from across the room. Court was right. Alex Harlow was on the make tonight.

"Good evening, Alex." Her voice was amazingly calm as she turned and leaned against the rail. He walked toward her, the black turtleneck and dark slacks helping him blend into the darkness around him. The heavy-lidded blue eyes found hers and held them as he advanced. There was a time, she reflected, when that look could have made her heart beat faster.

"You're looking lovely tonight," he said quietly, halting a couple of steps away. He said it the way he'd always said it, in a soft, seductive drawl that made it clear he knew when a woman had dressed for him. But she hadn't dressed for him tonight, Leya thought in silent amusement. She'd dressed for Court. The admission went almost unnoticed in the increasing excitement of the moment.

"Thank you," she replied demurely. "And where is your wife?"

"Haven't you heard?" Alex asked quietly. "We've split up."

"I'm sorry to hear that, since the two of you went to

such an effort to get together." If he caught the thread of sarcasm in her words, Alex didn't acknowledge it.

"Everyone makes mistakes, Leya." There was a slight pause. "I tried calling you earlier this week. There was no answer."

"I've been away for a few days," she replied, her arms stretched out on either side of her, resting on the cold metal railing as she lounged backward. The drink was clasped in the fingers of her right hand, half-empty.

"With him?"

"Him?" she questioned, eyes gleaming up at Alex's sardonically curved mouth.

"That man you came with tonight. From what I could see he appears to think he owns you."

"Does he?" she smiled.

"Don't be sarcastic, honey," Alex advised almost gently. "It isn't like you."

Leya's smile broadened. "Oh, I don't know about that. There are some who say I'm a natural shrew."

"Then they don't know you, do they?" he countered, stretching out his hand to stroke the side of her jaw with caressing fingers.

"Perhaps it's you who doesn't know me," she suggested, resisting the urge to pull her head away from his touch. God! Was it only a year ago she would have been thrilled?

"I know you," he stated with confidence, letting his fingers slip down further to tilt her chin. "I know you very well."

"Why did you try to call me this week, Alex?"

"Can't you guess?"

"Maybe. But I'd rather be sure," Leya whispered with a hint of invitation she knew he'd pick up immediately.

"When I first met you, Monica was the only thing on my mind."

"And I was a means to get to her?"

"Yes, I'm afraid so," he admitted in a tone that said he clearly expected her to forgive the deception. "It was only later that I realized what I'd thrown away in my efforts to win the wrong woman."

"Really?" Leya whispered skeptically. "When did you make that discovery?"

"You have gotten hard, Leya. Was it because of me? Because of what I did to you?"

She wanted to laugh and barely restrained the outburst. If he honestly thought she was acting uncharacteristically now, then it could only mean he'd never learned much about her true nature a year ago. But whose fault was that, she asked herself honestly. Hadn't she always been on her best behavior around Alex? She'd never fought with him, never given him the sharp edge of her tongue. Never, she suddenly realized, pushed the relationship to the point where they would have had to discover which of them was the stronger.

"Please don't feel guilty about my current attitude," she replied serenely, "I assure you I come by it naturally. You needn't take the blame for having turned me into a bitter woman. You might be interested to know that I'm really not bitter at all," she added, reflectively.

"Not even a little?" he pressed, bringing his face close to hers so that his mouth hovered an inch above her own. "I hurt you, Leya, didn't I? But I can make up for all that."

"How?" she asked simply, making no effort to pull away but feeling no great interest in the impending kiss. She viewed his mouth almost clinically.

"By starting over . . ." He kissed her slowly, lingeringly, with all the old expertise.

And Leya felt nothing at all except distaste. She stood very still, her arms still resting on the railing and waited for him to finish. How could she ever have been even mildly excited by his embrace, she wondered. But she knew the answer to that. It came as soon as Alex's arms went around her waist. Alex's kiss meant nothing now because she'd been exposed to Court Tremayne's lovemaking. It was Court her body craved, not Alex or any other man.

The realization was stunning and the problem it presented seemed overwhelming. But she would have to deal with it later. At the moment, it was Alex Harlow who held her and invited her with his caresses to restart an old romance. And it didn't seem quite fair that he should escape scot-free for the way he had treated her a year ago. He had made a fool of her and it seemed only appropriate that he should suffer the same experience. The possibility of revenge made Leya's eyes glitter with a hard platinum light.

"Do you want me back, Alex?" she asked dreamily, mouth curving softly as he lifted his head. "Is that the truth?"

He looked down into her uptilted face and she knew he saw only what he wanted to see there. He was convinced he had only to lift his finger and she would fall back into his arms.

"I think we would do very well together, Leya, my sweet," he whispered, his hands pressing her waist. She felt the beginnings of male arousal in him and was pleased. "This time we would start from scratch with no other woman involved. Yes, I want you back. Tonight. Come with me, Leya. I'll take you out to dinner and we can sort everything out between us."

"That sounds very pleasant, except for one thing," she murmured, her laughter threatening to well up and overflow.

"What's that?" he prodded persuasively, eyes gleaming.

"My fiancé." Leya dropped the small bombshell with no compunction whatsoever, glorying in the shock it had caused. "The man I'm with tonight. I'm in love, Alex, with a man who makes your kisses seem like cold dishwater. Looking at you now I can't even imagine what I ever thought I saw in you!"

"What the hell are you talking about?" he blazed, his hands falling away from her waist as if they had been burned. The blue eyes narrowed angrily.

"You heard the lady," said a hard, cold voice behind them.

Leya swung a momentarily startled glance over Alex's shoulder, her eyes colliding with Court's as he walked toward them. How long had he been standing in the shadows? she wondered frantically. What would he do? She prayed he would hold up his end of the deception, take the role he'd been assigned, and not ruin her small revenge.

"You two are engaged?" Alex demanded, stepping away from Leya and turning to face Court, who kept coming until he was close enough to slide an arm around Leya's waist.

"It was supposed to be something of a secret until we were ready to announce it, but I gather she couldn't resist telling you." Court turned his head to glance down at Leya as she stood tensely in the circle of his arm. He smiled with all the possessive warmth of a real fiancé, and she realized abruptly he was going to help her. Relief flowed through her veins, and confidence reheated her nervously cold body.

"Why didn't you say something earlier, Leya?" Alex snapped, his anger flaming as he caught sight of the laughter in her sparkling green eyes.

"I'm sorry, Alex," she apologized without any sign of contrition. "But you have to admit the opportunity was simply too good to pass up. If you could have seen the look on your face!"

"It was all a joke? Letting me kiss you like that?" he blazed, incensed.

"I'm afraid so. Why should I be interested in you after all this time, when I'm quite happily engaged to marry another man? Let's face it, Alex, we didn't exactly share an undying love!" Leya grinned, delighting in his reaction.

"You don't seem to mind having a fiancée who goes around kissing other men in the moonlight," Alex muttered to Court, clearly looking for a way of salvaging his pride. The two men faced each other across the short distance. Both were tall, but Court had a couple of inches on Alex. He also had a suggestion of strength that was lacking in the younger man. Strength and experience.

"From what I saw," Court replied in a leisurely tone, which was nonetheless menacing, "you were the one kissing her. Now that I *do* mind. In fact, you could say I take definite exception to that," he added lazily.

Leya felt the spring-tight tension in Court through the sinewy arm that crushed her against him. He was angry but he was in complete control.

"How do you know it wasn't her fault?" Alex mocked bitterly, sliding an accusing look at Leya's cheerfully smiling face. His eyes hardened at the humor in her. There was no worse way to hurt a man than to laugh at him, she thought.

"Oh, I know Leya well enough to know what she's like when she's enjoying a kiss," Court informed him with a cool certainty that left no doubt in his listeners' minds that he had Leya's physical reactions well catalogued. Leya would have blushed but for the fact that she was having too much fun.

"Is that so?" Alex began aggressively. "Well, let me tell you I knew her a long time before you came along and I . . ."

"One more word and I'll throw you over the railing," Court interrupted with distinct intent. "Now why don't you take your humiliation like a man and slink off somewhere? I promise to keep Leya away from you in the future. You needn't be afraid she'll exercise her claws on you again."

"Goodnight, Alex," Leya chimed in at once. "So nice to see you again. I enjoyed it immensely."

"Why, you little—"

"I know it's a temptation, but don't say it," Court advised. "You know how it is—if you actually say it, I'll have to do something about it."

Without a word, Alex swung furiously off into the night, heading toward the doors opening onto the terrace. In a few seconds, he had disappeared.

For a moment, silence reigned under the cold night sky, and then Leya tried to take a sip from the glass she was still clutching in her right hand. But it was no use—the laughter bubbled over and spilled out, making it impossible to swallow.

"Oh, Court," she grinned, twisting to look up into his face. "How can I ever thank you? That was fabulous! Did you see the look on his face? He was positively livid!"

"Enjoy yourself, Leya?" he asked laconically, his arm still wrapping her close. Once again, he removed the glass from her fingers, setting it down on the railing this time.

"Enormously," she assured him, deciding not to make an issue out of his insistence on taking the drink away from her. She was feeling much too charitable at the moment. "And it wouldn't have had nearly the effect without you showing up when you did. Perfect timing!"

"Thank you. I'd been standing there for some time, you see, trying to decide when to make my appearance," he murmured, his rugged features cast in an unreadable expression as he gazed down at her gleaming silver-green eyes.

"Well, you chose an excellent moment. I'm very appreciative. That man deserved everything he got and more. Would you have really thrown him over the railing if he'd insulted me?"

"Yes, I think so," he said calmly.

"Terribly energetic," she pointed out.

"There are occasions in life when one must bestir oneself and put forth the effort," he observed. "Are you really feeling quite grateful for my assistance, Leya Brandon?" he added, taking a sip from his own glass.

"Oh, yes," she assured him cheerfully enough. She could feel the effects of the alcohol in her bloodstream, but she didn't feel drunk, merely pleasantly high.

"Grateful enough to let my help with your revenge this evening cancel out the grudge you're holding against me?" He waited for her response, a quirking smile on his hard mouth.

"What are you talking about?" she whispered, sobering quickly and twisting enough to put some space between the two of them. He didn't try to stop her.

"I'm talking about forgiving me for that business with the contract and letting our relationship go back to where it was before you found out who I was."

"You think you've made up for what you did by helping me out tonight?" Her voice was husky and there was a new pounding in her veins that wasn't induced by alcohol. She was remembering the lesson she'd learned in Alex's arms a few minutes earlier. The lesson had taught her that it was Court's embraces she wanted. Court's . . . love?

Dear lord! Was she going to be an even greater fool and fall in love with the man? Leya screamed silently. She saw the way he was watching her, waiting for her to say that the score between them was settled. How did he truly feel about her? How could any woman know whether a man like this had genuinely fallen for her or whether he was still interested only in controlling a potentially difficult unknown quantity?

And how could she ever learn the answer to that

question unless she took the risk of giving him another chance?

"I think you owe me a great deal for what I let you do tonight," he said quietly, deliberately pressing his case.

"You mean for using you?"

"Wasn't that what it amounted to?" he retorted with an edge on his words.

"I suppose so," she acknowledged.

"Come on, Leya. You can be more honest than that!"

"All right, so I used you a bit. What harm did it do?"

"None, but I want some payment for the privilege, and I think forgiving me for the way you feel I treated you in Oregon is little enough recompense."

She glared at him, trying to sort through her chaotic emotions. Could they start over? Had he really begun to feel something important for her?

"And if I said we were even?" she hedged carefully.

"Then we could take up where we left off. Get to know each other better . . ."

She eyed him speculatively. "Is that what you want?"

"Yes, it's what I want."

Was he telling the truth or was he still worried about the threat she represented to his control of Brandon Security? But she sensed that his desire for her, at least, was honest. Could they build something lasting out of such a fleeting emotion? All her instincts urged her to take the risk of finding out. She could never be satisfied with herself or with life if she didn't seek to know the true limits of this relationship.

The sudden knowledge answered all her questions. She would take the challenge and the risk of discovering the truth about his feelings for her.

Warily, as if she were reentering the lists for another round of combat, Leya inclined her head once and whispered, "Yes, Court. I'm willing to start over again. That is," she added in a small voice, "if it's true that you deceived me because you really wanted to pursue our relationship and not just to get my signature on the contract."

"It's the truth, Leya," he told her huskily.

He stepped forward, sweeping her into his arms. "Leya, my maddening little shrew. I know how you must have felt when you discovered I'd deceived you. I would have felt the same. But I was so sure that once I had you in my bed nothing else would matter! I'm glad you've had your revenge by using me. We can put it all behind us. I handled you all wrong, I know that now. You're a lot like me, and I should have . . ."

"There you two are!" Keith's voice called cheerfully into the darkness. "We were wondering where you'd disappeared. I take it everything is settled? I'll have to hand it to you, Court! You sure know how to tie up loose ends!"

There was a distinctly admiring note in his voice. One that finally made Leya lift her head from Court's shoulder in sudden alertness.

Still clasped in Court's arms, which had tightened at the sound of Keith's words, she looked past the massive shoulder and directly into her brother's smiling gaze.

"What are you talking about?" she demanded, in a tone of voice she hadn't used on him since eighth grade, when she'd finally learned little brothers were more easily handled with cajolery than threats, especially when they started getting bigger than their sisters.

"Your, er, relationship with Court, here," Keith

returned, picking up some of the vibrations but not yet paying them sufficient heed. "The last thing Court said to me before slamming out of the office to find you at that inn up in Oregon was that he had an awful premonition he'd been fated to tame the green-eyed witch who was laughing at him from the picture on my office wall. He said the one sure way to control a troublesome female was in bed. I'll admit I didn't expect an engagement so quickly. But Alex Harlow is telling everyone . . ."

Keith broke off, grinning at his sister's stunned expression. "Haven't you learned yet, sister dear, that the only thing that prompts Court out of his easy chair or his workshop is a challenge? He'll do whatever he has to do in order to win. Why do you think I wanted him on the side of Brandon Security?"

"A challenge," Leya repeated, the metal in her eyes glowing with white heat as she stepped back out of Court's slackening embrace to face him.

"That's what this has been about all along, hasn't it? You *did* come up to that inn in Oregon intending to seduce me because that seemed like the easiest way to overcome the challenge I represented. You didn't take one look at me and suddenly decide our relationship was more important than the contract. You established a relationship in order to get that damned document signed! To control me!"

"Leya, listen to me," he began determinedly. "You've got it all wrong! Your brother doesn't know what the hell he's talking about. You and I—"

"No, he doesn't. He automatically assumed you were planning to marry me," she exploded violently. "Me, I know better. I know you'd never get *that* carried away with a mere challenge. An amusing little affair, during which you made certain I kept my interfering hands off Brandon Security, would be more to your taste, wouldn't it? Well, just in case you're not getting enough excitement out of the diversion, let me spice things up a bit!"

With that, Leya grabbed the half-full glass standing on the railing and hurled the contents at his yellow shirt. As the alcohol and ice soaked him, she whirled and walked off the terrace.

Chapter Six

*H*er exit scene lacked only a small touch of practicality to keep it from being perfect, Leya reflected a moment later as she swept into the party and realized she didn't have a convenient ride home.

It was the little things that could so easily trip one up in life! In disgust, Leya grabbed a drink off a passing tray, reminding herself she hadn't been allowed to finish one yet, thanks to Court. She was making her way over to a far corner of the room, where it might have been possible to stay out of sight until her brother reappeared from the terrace, when Susan Adams glided up to her. Why were half the women in California blonde?

"I was wondering where you'd hidden yourself, Leya." Susan's eyes were lit with an interest that didn't fool Leya for a second.

"I've hidden Court outside on the terrace," Leya

told her sweetly. "But as you can see, I'm not the least bit hard to find. Don't worry, Susan, I'm sure he'll be back in a moment." The thought bred an unpleasant anticipation in Leya's own mind, however. What was she going to do when he returned from the terrace and came gunning for her?

There wasn't much he could do to her in a room full of people, she told herself bravely and wondered exactly how much her own brother would be on her side. Keith's admiration for his newfound mentor seemed very high. So high that he was happy to consider Court as a brother-in-law! Of course, that event was unlikely in the extreme, Leya thought glumly, taking a swallow of her drink. Court might bestir himself for a challenge, but something told her he had enough sense of self-preservation to keep from being so caught up in the battle that he'd go to those lengths!

"He's a very fascinating man, your fiancé," Susan was saying chattily, her bright eyes on Leya's brooding expression. "I must say the news came as a surprise, though. I had no idea . . ."

"My what?" Leya knew she sounded almost as startled at the statement as Alex had earlier. She frowned at Susan.

"Isn't it public knowledge yet?" Susan murmured with totally false anxiety. "I'm sorry if I wasn't supposed to know, but frankly the whole room will know fairly soon. Rumors like this get around a party quickly, and several people here know you or your brother . . ."

"Who told you that I was engaged to Court?"

"Alex Harlow. You remember him?" Susan's

prompting on the name was quite unnecessary, Leya thought. She was well aware of what had happened a year ago. "He seemed very upset about something and left a few minutes ago. You wouldn't know why he was angry, would you?" she added hopefully. Susan loved to know details.

"Haven't the foggiest," Leya retorted dryly. "As for this engagement business," she began, intending to squelch the stupid rumor as quickly as possible. She was interrupted before the blow could be dealt.

"Leya! Just heard the news! Congratulations. That tall man with the bedroom eyes is the one, I take it?" Alice Compton came forward, a sandy-haired escort in tow. Alice's cheerful expression was full of genuine goodwill.

"Bedroom eyes!" Leya exclaimed vengefully. "Court doesn't have bedroom eyes. That sort of narrowed, sultry look is a sign of chronic laziness, not passion!" For the life of her, she didn't know what made her say that, but the impulse was irresistible.

"I resent that," murmured a familiar gravelly voice behind her, as Court's hand snaked around her waist and removed the glass from her hand. "Let's go home, little Leya, and we'll find out exactly which emotion you're seeing in my eyes!"

The laughter of those who heard the remark covered Leya's gritted exclamation. She turned to lift mocking liquid eyes up to his. "I wouldn't want to put you to the effort, darling," she purred.

"Don't fret, sweetheart," he returned with a patently insincere assurance, "I've been fortifying myself at Susan's buffet table. I think I can work up the energy!"

Under cover of more laughter from those around them, Leya bared her teeth in the parody of a charming smile. She confronted the deep, warning gleam in the tortoiseshell eyes and felt the overall intent in him as if it were a tangible electrical charge. He made no move to touch her but the threat in him was blatant.

"Oh, dear," she observed nastily. "Did you have an accident with your drink?" Her eyes ran mockingly over the dampened shirt front. A mixture of excitement and anger raced along her nerve endings as their confrontation began to escalate.

"Would you believe it? I seem to have gotten in the path of a young lady who'd imbibed a little too much this evening. But that's all right. I've got a dry shirt at home. Are you ready to leave?"

"No, I'm not," Leya murmured in satisfaction. "Unlike the poor young woman whose path you crossed, I haven't had a chance to imbibe too much. I haven't had a chance to finish even one drink tonight!"

"Pity," he drawled heartlessly. "But if I'm going to make the effort to overcome my chronic laziness tonight, then the least you can do is try and keep from passing out on me!" His meaning was abundantly clear.

Keith's voice interrupted over the ensuing roar of laughter from a gathering crowd. He pushed his way toward where his sister and Court were faced off, his green eyes laughing. Blonde little Angie was beginning to sulk at the lack of attention she was receiving, Leya had time to note.

"Are you two going to stand there and make a scene instead of officially announcing the engagement?"

"Yes!" Leya gritted willingly. She could think of

nothing more satisfying in that moment than a knock-down, drag-out scene in which she was the undisputed victor! Her eyes never left her opponent's face as he growled his answer almost simultaneously.

"No," Court said quite clearly. "We are going to make the announcement and then go home and conduct our scene!"

"I certainly hope you enjoy giving a performance on your own, because I intend to stay right here at the party!"

"Leya, my charming wife-to-be," Court said with vast politeness, "I will give you a choice: You may leave this party on my arm or over my shoulder. Take your pick!"

She felt the threat in him, but Leya's own emotions were vibrating at too high a pitch to care. The platinum sheen in her eyes clashed with the molten gold in his and she smiled dangerously.

"Is that a multiple-choice question?" she asked interestedly.

"It is."

"Then I choose 'none of the above!'" Leya whirled away, intent only on getting out of range as quickly as possible. But the amused crowd hemmed her in, trapping her very conveniently for Court, who didn't hesitate.

"I'll bet," he offered as his hand struck, encircling the small bones of her wrist like a manacle, "that you never did very well on multiple-choice tests in school!"

Leya gave a squeak of very real alarm as she felt herself yanked off balance. Before she could clutch at something, anything, she felt the impact of Court's shoulder in her stomach and then she was staring down his back at the floor, her heavy braid falling past her head.

For an instant, the wind was knocked out of her and, unable to protest, she heard her captor speak quite matter-of-factly to the roomful of people.

"You'll excuse us, I'm sure, while I take Leya home, so that one of us can beat the other into submission in private!"

Leya gulped air as Court began striding for the door.

"Keith!" she cried furiously. "Do something!" Desperately, she tried to twist her head high enough to see her brother, who spread his hands helplessly.

"What can I do, Leya? The man has an iron-clad contract to do just about anything he likes with Brandon Security!" The laughter in him was pure Brandon. "And you signed it yourself!"

"I'm not part of Brandon Security!" she charged ominously, knowing she had been carried almost as far as the door.

"Yes, you are," Court corrected as he put his free hand on the knob. "You're the silent partner, remember?"

"Damn you!" Then, knowing she needed the last word before the door closed, she said to the ring of delighted faces, "For the record, there is no engagement!" The last memory of the party was that of Keith's laughing eyes.

But her own silver-green gaze contained no humor at all as Court dumped her unceremoniously into the front seat of his car a moment later, slamming the door as she righted herself. He was sliding in beside her on the opposite side of the car before Leya had straightened up and found the door handle. He turned in the seat, filling the whole front cockpit with his strength and will, or so it seemed to Leya. His arm stretched out along the back of the seat, his hand resting threateningly behind her head as she twisted to face him.

"How dare you?" she choked, her fury and humiliation rising up like a tide. "How could you do a thing like that to me? You had absolutely no right to drag me off like that and . . . and make a fool of me! Again!"

"You asked for everything you got, Leya Brandon," he bit out and she abruptly realized there was no laughter in him, either. Their scene at the party might have amused the bystanders, but the two participants were in deadly earnest, locked in a battle that had escalated to major proportions.

"Only from your point of view," she spat. "Personally, I see myself as an innocent victim!"

"Shrews are never innocent victims! I'm still damp from that drink you threw all over me in a fit of temper, remember! And after all I'd just done for you, too!" he added, plainly outraged. In the darkness of the cold car, his eyes gleamed down at her.

"All *you* had just done! You've got your nerve! You simply walked into a private scene between me and another man . . ."

"Walked in just in time to hear you making use of me to revenge yourself on said other individual! Talk about nerve, Leya, you don't seem to be lacking in it! I heard you tell Harlow you were in love with me, that my kisses made his seem like cold dishwater. That's called playing one man off against another, little witch, and I don't like being part of your games! I was willing to tolerate it so you could have your revenge on me, too, but . . ."

"Tolerate it! You did a hell of a lot more than tolerate it! What did you hope to accomplish by letting everyone think we're lovers? Was it all part of the challenge, Court? The challenge I seem to represent to you? I can see how it all started, naturally. First, you were annoyed when I didn't meekly show up at the meeting you'd arranged so that you could browbeat me into signing that contract. Then, after you'd tricked me into signing it, you couldn't satisfy your damn male ego, which only knows one kind of victory over a woman. I realized what was happening before you got me into bed and that really annoyed you, didn't it? Made the challenge all the greater, didn't it? Then, tonight you deliberately came to my rescue and backed up my story to Alex. That gave you the opening you needed to renew your campaign to polish off your big win at Brandon Security! And I, like the complete fool I've shown myself to be lately, fell for it. I actually let you talk me into giving our relationship another chance!"

"You've got it all figured out in your own brilliantly twisted fashion, don't you?" he grated. Out of the corner of her eye, Leya saw the hand resting beside her head close into a fist.

"Go ahead and deny it if you can! The only thing I don't understand is why the hints of marriage to Keith? Why let him think you're serious? But I suppose those were just tactics, weren't they? Little flanking maneuvers to push me in the right direction?"

"Which happens to be my bed! And that's where you're going to wind up, sooner or later, Leya my shrew," he flung back, "because you know what I think? I think you were telling Alex Harlow the truth tonight, even if you were using it for your own purposes!"

"What the hell are you saying?" she blazed, infuriated anew.

"I think you are in love with me! I think you fell in love with me back in Oregon!"

"In only two days?" she scoffed, secretly appalled at his analysis. "Not likely!"

"What does time have to do with it? I could have taken you that night you signed the contract and you know it! I could have done it the next day, even though you were furious at me. When I held you and touched you on the beach, you were responding in spite of yourself!"

"You'd like to think that's the truth, wouldn't you? That I'd actually be so overcome by your mastery of seduction I'd fall in love with you regardless of what you did to me! Much more satisfying than just getting me into bed and more efficient, too! A woman in love is probably a lot easier to control than one who will merely consent to go to bed with you. That would give you a hell of a victory, wouldn't it?"

"Leya, you're becoming totally unreasonable. I'm taking you home!" Court threw himself around in the seat, shoving the key into the ignition and slamming the expensive car into gear.

Leya could read the fury in him and the control he was exerting over it. It radiated out to every corner of the vehicle.

"Thank you," she bit out icily. "Home is precisely where I want to go!"

In the dimly lit interior, she saw him lift one heavy eyebrow but he said nothing. She sat in frozen silence as he drove with an economy of movement and wished her own self-control wasn't so weak.

Oh, the anger was a bracing enough emotion, but the slight trembling in her lower lip was caused by another feeling entirely, one she didn't want to acknowledge but which forced itself on her awareness. Leya was far too honest to pretend she didn't understand what her mind and body were crying out. For a while, there on the terrace this evening she had wanted very badly to say the score between herself and Court was even, to declare a truce and start over. And Court was smart, too smart not to guess that for a few moments he had been close to getting what he wanted.

But why? she wondered bitterly. What kind of man would get so intrigued by the kind of challenge she represented? What kind of man needed to assert his victory over a woman by dragging her off to bed? The answer had to be only a man who knew his victory wasn't secure.

"Where are we going?" she suddenly demanded suspiciously.

"I told you, I'm taking you home. My apartment. You wouldn't want me to catch cold in this damp shirt, would you?" he added mockingly.

"It won't take that much extra time to drop me off at my home, first!"

"Heartless creature," he murmured, not changing direction.

"Court!"

"Leya," he sighed. "We're going to talk this out

126

tonight and my apartment is the logical place to do that."

"Afraid of giving me the home-court advantage?" she snapped.

"I suppose," he nodded wryly. "Maybe I'll feel safer on my own turf. I've had it with your crazy reasoning processes. To think I once thought you an intelligent woman!"

"Your insults don't bother me, Court," she managed tightly. "Perhaps if you think I'm not too bright you'll lose interest in the game!"

"I'm not the one who wants to play games, Leya, but if you force me into them I can guarantee I'll play to win."

"Your threats don't bother me any more than your insults!"

"In that case, you've got a lot to learn." But he sounded calmer now, as if he were determined to be reasonable in the face of a totally unreasonable woman's tirade.

He also sounded implacable, and although she made a few more attempts to talk him out of it, Leya knew with great certainty that he wasn't going to take her back to her own house until he'd had his say on his own territory.

The ride was concluded in chilly silence. When at last Court drew the car into the parking lot of an exclusive condominium complex, Leya finally roused herself sufficiently to note caustically, "I thought you said you had an apartment."

"I'm renting one of the condos from the owner." He shrugged. "It feels like an apartment."

The thick, verdant landscaping lent privacy to the individual units of the complex. The condominiums were modern, typically Californian in style with cedar siding, interesting angles, and a great many windows. Not at all as cozy and welcoming as her own home, Leya decided smugly.

"Come on, let's get inside. I'm cold." Court switched off the engine, heading around to Leya's side of the car but failing to arrive in time to assist her.

He said nothing about her obvious desire to ignore the intended courtesy, merely taking her arm firmly in his and leading her up the flagstone path.

"I can't imagine what else you have to say this evening," she grumbled as he silently opened the front door and ushered her into a pleasant but, to her eyes, uninspiring living room.

"Why don't we simply call the whole thing quits?" she added, taking in the politely neutral cream-colored carpeting, the bland but expensive beige-and-tan modern furniture and the touches of teakwood in the end tables. "You've won the basic prize by getting me to sign that contract. Have the grace to be content with the major victory!"

"What?" he demanded with the first hint of humor since they had left the party. "And imply you aren't as important a victory as the contract was? I wouldn't think of insulting you so!"

"Why not? You've already insulted me by telling me I'm not particularly bright." Leya chose one of the rounded tan chairs near the fireplace and flung herself into it with unconscious grace. Arms stretched out along the curving back, she crossed her legs with deliberate elegance and disdain and eyed him coolly.

"But you know that really isn't true, don't you? And therefore it was very ineffective as a slander. I only said it out of annoyance," he told her dismissingly, his eyes following her movements.

Leya gritted her teeth. "Why should you be annoyed at a challenge, Court? My brother says it's the only thing that gets you excited in life!"

"Where does everyone get this notion that I'm attracted to difficult problems?" he demanded, lifting golden-brown eyes toward heaven in a beseeching gesture.

"Aren't you?" Leya ground out, gazing at him morosely from under her lashes.

"Not in my private life," he retorted feelingly, coming across the room with a slow, stalking stride.

"Nonsense," she shot back caustically. "A challenge is a challenge. Tell me about this flaw in your character, Court Tremayne. What is it with the idea of a challenge? Were you the kind of little kid who couldn't resist a dare?"

"If we're going to get involved in a discussion of my childhood, you'll have to excuse me while I change my shirt, first." His hands went to the buttons of the yellow fabric and Leya glanced pointedly away. "Why don't you make us some tea while I, er, slip into something more comfortable. I think you'll find everything you need in the kitchen." He paused. "And stop looking at the furniture that way. It's not mine. It came with the condo."

He turned and walked out of the living room, leaving her to do as she liked about the tea. Fingers drumming on the arms of the chair, Leya considered the options and decided to make the beverage. She'd *known* the furniture hadn't been his, she told herself wryly. She had the feeling his normal décor would be a lot more like her own: bright, positive, and warm.

The condo kitchen was as sleek and modern as the rest of the place. A copper teakettle sat invitingly on the almond-colored stove, and with very little rummaging, she found the teacups. They were conveniently near the stove, exactly where she kept her own at home. She and Court even organized alike!

"There," he informed her, walking back into the living room a few minutes later buttoning a dry shirt, "that's better. Now I can discuss my character flaw without danger of catching cold!"

Leya set the tea things down on one of the teak tables and watched as he knelt in front of the fireplace and began to stack kindling.

"Perhaps talking about it will help you work it out," she agreed sweetly, too sweetly.

"You're very kind. I don't think you're asking out of anything more than clinical interest, but I'll try and explain, anyway," he sighed, striking a match and bending his head momentarily over the flame.

There was a pause while he lit the fire, and then he sat back on his heels, studying the blaze intently until he was sure it had caught. He rose with a lithe grace that appealed to Leya's senses in spite of her mood, and sank into the chair across from her. He stretched his legs out in front of himself, slumping into the cushions and regarding her with a brooding air.

"About your lifelong problem," she prompted acidly.

"Oh, yes, my passion for challenge," he groaned, reaching for his tea. "You were wrong about me being the kind of little kid who's always accepting a dare, you know."

"Really?" Leya's voice held only cool, polite interest.

"I was an only child, you see, and I never did enjoy playing with other kids. Much preferred the pleasure of my own company. I wasn't antisocial, you understand," he put in with mock reassurance. "Just not interested in a lot of the things that amused my contemporaries. I liked to spend my free time in the basement with my tools and my electronics."

Leya half-smiled in spite of herself. The image was all too familiar. "Did your parents worry about your preference for solitude?"

"No," he chuckled. "Did yours?" He smiled at her with keen perception.

"No, I was lucky," she admitted. "Mom and Dad seemed to understand. They were kind enough to let me curl up alone with my books and my rock polisher!"

"Rock polisher?" He grinned.

"I had a little lapidary shop in my corner of the basement. It's how I became interested in jewelry making. But we were discussing your problems, I believe," she added determinedly. She was not about to let him charm her tonight!

"Well, where was I?" he said, leaning his head back in the chair.

"Your basement."

"Yes. I had a ham radio set up down there and all sorts of electrical test equipment. I used to send off for those build-it-yourself kits, and then one day . . ."

"You built it yourself without a kit?"

"How did you guess?"

"It was inevitable."

"Perhaps," he nodded quietly. "At any rate, I began having more fun tinkering and putting odd things together on my own than building from a set of plans. But when it came time to go off to college, it wasn't engineering that intrigued me, it was finance. Creative finance, as they say. I was attracted to the things that could be done when money was cleverly applied. The two interests, electronics and finance, sort of flowed together."

"Where did you go to college?"

"Berkeley."

"You were born in California?" Leya prodded, interested even though she knew she ought to be just the opposite.

"Umm. I was raised in a little town on the San Francisco peninsula. How about you?"

"Here in Santa Rosa," she confided. "But I chose the University of California campus in Santa Barbara when it came time to go off to school. Berkeley always seemed much too big, too urban for my tastes."

"Your choice doesn't surprise me," he told her softly, eyes warming. "The Santa Barbara campus would be a good setting for you, being right on the ocean. You seem to have an affinity for windswept beaches . . ."

For a charged moment, the memories of Oregon hung between them, and then Leya deliberately pushed them aside.

"The beaches there were nice, but the degree in English was quite useless!" She smiled. "Until, that is, I took some business courses. I had never been particularly interested in business, but I found I did rather well. By the time I graduated, I had decided I was the entrepreneurial sort."

"The bookstore?"

"Dad lent me the money to get started." Leya smiled suddenly. "Said he had complete faith in the Brandon talent for making money. I paid him back, too. Within a year the store was making money and now it brings in a very nice income. I'm thinking of opening up a branch out at the new shopping center."

"You weren't interested in taking over your father's business?"

"No, I'm much too independent. I'd never work well in a large managerial setting, even if I were the boss. Too many other people to consider. I think Keith will do it well, though. He likes directing others and pulling a team together."

"I agree, and when I've shown him a few of the ropes regarding finance and marketing . . ."

"We seem to have lost the train of thought here," she interrupted smoothly. "How *did* you come to be such an authority, anyhow?"

He shrugged. "When I graduated, it soon became apparent that I was never going to be happy working nine-to-five for someone else."

"Not enough *challenge* in the daily grind of engineering and accounting?"

"I wish you would stop using that word," he complained good-naturedly, his eyes laughing at her. Leya felt herself slipping dangerously back under the spell of the easy camaraderie they had discovered in Oregon. She must keep her distance tonight, she warned herself severely.

"Think of a better word," she invited pointedly.

"In any event," he began firmly, "it became obvious that my attention span was relatively short when it came to the mundane things of life, such as holding a regular job. So I started working on a contract basis."

"Choosing only the most interesting little puzzles to work on?" Leya drawled knowingly.

"Well, there's not much point in picking and choosing contracts unless one selects only the most interesting and profitable, is there?" he countered quellingly. "Besides, contract work gave me time for my basement tinkering."

"What's the longest contract you've ever accepted?" Leya demanded, eyes narrowing.

"This one," he answered honestly. "The idea of trying to help save Brandon Security and get a piece of the action if I was successful represented an interesting—" He broke off, wincing.

"An interesting challenge?" she supplied helpfully, watching him demurely over the rim of her cup.

"Vicious little thing, aren't you?"

"What do you do when you're not busy confronting the current challenge?"

"Lapse back into happy isolation in a basement or spare room somewhere," he admitted promptly. "Or head for the solitude of a beach. Just like you."

Leya ignored the bid to draw a parallel with herself. "What about the blondes you mentioned at the party? Do you drag them down into your basement or to the beach?"

"I wondered when we'd get around to them," he chuckled.

"I'm asking when do *you* get around to them?" she retorted.

. "Whenever the mood comes over me!"

"Do you see each new one as a challenge?" Leya asked kindly, incredibly irritated at his admission.

"Hardly," he quipped blandly. "My women tend to be in the same category as your Alex Harlow. Pretty but rather self-centered and not too bright."

"Have you ever married one of them?" Leya couldn't resist the question. At his age, it would be quite natural if he'd been married.

There was a distinct pause while Court considered his answer. "I came damn close once," he finally admitted softly. "We were engaged before I realized my mistake."

"What was the mistake, Court?" Leya pressed tightly. "Almost succumbing to a challenge?"

"My mistake," he told her flatly, eyes narrowed, "was in thinking she was different from the others. I was lucky. I found out in time she wasn't. She wanted what the others wanted, but she was better at disguising her goals than most."

"What happened?" Leya hated herself for asking, but she couldn't stifle her curiosity.

"She thought I was going to be offered the chief executive position at the firm for which I was working at the time."

"And?"

"And I was," he said simply. "But I declined. When she found out, she declined me."

"Were you very hurt?" Leya asked tentatively, astonished at the wave of compassion for him which suddenly moved her.

"My pride more than anything. When I realized that, I also realized I'd had a very narrow escape!"

"And you've been cautious since then, right?" she hazarded, smiling gently. "Stuck to the nonchallenging blondes who are easy to handle?"

The flash of mutual understanding that passed between them was impossible to ignore. Leya knew exactly what Court had felt when he discovered he had been used. She'd been through it with Alex. Court proved he was on the same wavelength when his eyes met hers directly and he said softly, "Is that so different from what you've been doing since Harlow?"

"What do you know about what I've been doing since I dated Alex?"

"Your brother told me. He said you've been seeing a string of easily managed types who do exactly as they're bid or find themselves out of the running."

"I'll have to speak to my brother. He clearly has no feeling for family loyalty," Leya sighed irritably.

"Is it true?" Court probed.

"What if it is?" she returned aloofly, chin lifting. "Can you blame me for not wanting to get burned again?"

"No, I've been just as cautious," he murmured soothingly. "I always make it a point to find out the price first now. I didn't like being used, either. Maybe we've both been waiting for the right, uh, challenge."

"Court!" The tension in the room suddenly elevated again.

"I'm only teasing you, honey," he said quickly. "Couldn't you please take pity on a basically peaceful, leisurely male who wants a peaceful, leisurely relationship with you?"

He looked so persuasively pleading that Leya almost forgot herself. Then her lower lip firmed.

"Everything you've told me so far only points up the fact that whatever attraction I hold for you is on the level of a . . . a novelty," she whispered dejectedly. "I think my brother was right. When you get involved in a suitable challenge you like to win. Somehow, in your mind I've become part of the challenge of Brandon Security, and you want to make sure I'm under your control. Are you afraid I'll try and turn my brother against you? Or use my shares to block your decisions?"

"That's got nothing to do with it!" he glowered. "How many times do I have to tell you this is strictly between you and me?"

"I might have believed you if my brother hadn't come out on the terrace when he did tonight. But hearing him describe you storming out of his office when you found out I wasn't showing up for the meeting and that—that awful remark about controlling women by taking them to bed! How do you expect me to believe you after hearing all that? It's clear you saw me as a thorn in your side. A woman you're determined to bring to heel the only way you know how. It's no use, Court, you're not going to talk me into bed!"

He set the teacup down on the end table with a warning clatter.

"You are a stubborn, illogical little shrew, and I've had it with trying to reason with you tonight!"

He was on his feet with an electric movement that was much too fast for a man who didn't believe in athletic endeavors.

Before she could safely set down her teacup and leap to her feet, he was reaching for her wrist and pulling her up in front of him.

"Let me go, Court. If you can't conduct a civilized conversation, then you may as well take me home!" With a regal tilt of her dark head, she indicated the door. "I'm sure you'll understand my stubborn, illogical reasons for wanting you to do so!"

The tortoiseshell eyes were alive with male purpose, and his hold tightened on her wrist.

"I'm not taking you anywhere except into my bedroom," he drawled. "If we can't communicate verbally, we'll rely on more primitive techniques!"

Chapter Seven

"Court, this has gone far enough," Leya declared forcefully, calling on her total reserve of willpower. "You've done nothing but manhandle me this evening and I've had it!"

"You're telling me!" he agreed with heavy mockery, ignoring her attempt to free her wrists. "You're determined to run me to a frazzle, aren't you?" he went on accusingly, his face very close to hers, his eyes sweeping over her parted lips. "I've told you time and again I'm not a terribly energetic man. Why do you do this to me?"

"You're the one who started it!" she gasped, infuriated and desperately trying to retain some semblance of self-control. "You insist on playing the heavy-handed male and then wonder why I object!"

"You force me into that role because you keep playing the part of the recalcitrant, willful female."

"You forget," she charged defiantly, "that's my main attraction for you! If I turned meek and willing, you'd probably lose interest immediately!"

"Is that why you behave this way?" he asked, as if understanding had just dawned. "You're trying to hold my attention?" He looked very pleased.

"No!" she stormed, incensed that he had deliberately misunderstood her.

"Then why don't you try being meek and willing and see if that succeeds in getting rid of me?" he suggested helpfully.

"Because by the time I found out whether or not that would work it would be a trifle too late!"

"I've got news for you, honey," he retorted, stooping to swing her high into his arms. "It's already too late. Much too late."

"Court!" Leya was clamped tightly to his broad chest, and the heat of him threatened to burn her fingertips through the material of his shirt. "Put me down this instant! I will not be . . . be carried off for your amusement!"

"When you discover something amusing in all this," he told her encouragingly, striding toward the hall, "let me know. Personally, I'm not laughing."

"I'll never forgive you!" she tried valiantly as he rounded the corner with due caution for her head.

But already she could feel the excitement churning in her veins, almost swamping her with its intensity. She didn't want it to be like this, not with so much unresolved between them. But she couldn't deny to herself that she wanted him. She had wanted him since their meeting in Oregon. And she was very much afraid it was amounting to something much deeper and more dangerous. With feelings this chaotic, was love very far away?

"You already forgave me earlier this evening out on that terrace," he pointed out, kicking open the bedroom door with a careless foot. "You said we could take up where we left off in Oregon. This, in case you've forgotten, is where we left off!"

"Not quite!" she hissed as he tossed her down lightly onto a wide, low bed and flipped on the small lamp standing on the bedstand. "We were still getting to know each other. We weren't sleeping together!"

The room was as sleek and modern and neutrally colored as the rest of the condominium. Low-profile teak furniture and cream-colored carpeting and drapes were relieved by a suitably modern abstract painting hanging over the bed. The quilt on which she lay was a fat, fluffy goosedown affair that had probably cost a fortune. Too bad it had been done in beige. A part of Leya insisted it would have looked much better in a vibrant red.

"We weren't sleeping together only because you hadn't gotten around to admitting you really wanted me," he drawled, baiting her with a caressing, knowing glance as he straightened. "But now that you've crossed that hurdle—"

"I never admitted that!" she almost screeched, nails digging into the quilt. At least not out loud, she added in silent justification.

"Yes, you did. I distinctly heard you tell Alex Harlow that you were in love with me and that you planned to marry me," he reminded her with deep satisfaction.

"That's the main reason I refrained from throwing him over the rail, you know. I decided you'd done a good enough job of punishing him for daring to kiss you."

"You beast! You know I only said that to get some revenge! I didn't mean it!" But how much of it had she meant? The words she had used so easily to revenge herself on Alex had come quite readily to her tongue. It was easy to say she was in love with Court. Too easy.

"You can say it again tonight, then," he told her agreeably. "And this time you can mean it!"

She watched, wide-eyed, as he began unbuttoning his shirt. The sight had a certain mesmerizing quality that caught at her senses. When he started on the cuffs, the shirt front now hanging open and revealing the dark mat of hair on his chest, Leya finally summoned the will to move.

She flung herself without any warning to the far side of the bed. But fast as she was, Court was even faster, diving across the low, wide bed and snagging her around the waist before she could get to her feet.

"My God!" he breathed, aggrieved, "why didn't someone tell me taming shrews was such hard work? If this keeps up much longer, I'll need a rest cure!"

"Damn you!" Leya wailed as he hauled her down, pinning her beneath him and using his weight to crush her gently into the quilt. "Isn't there any way of making you see reason?"

"Stop fighting me," he whispered, his voice deepening as his gaze burned over her. "I can be a very reasonable man. All I ask from you tonight is the truth, or at least a portion of it."

"What portion?" she hissed scathingly, already violently aware of the warmth and weight of him as it overwhelmed her senses.

"At least admit that you want me!"

His hands gently caught her wrists and pinned them on either side of her head, his mouth hovered an inch above her lips. Leya's breath was beginning to come more quickly as her nerves registered the impact of him.

"You mean give you the victory you want," she corrected dismally.

"Think of it any way you like," he rasped. "Just stop fighting me long enough to let me show you how good it will be between us!"

Leya watched him in the soft light, her eyes heated emeralds as the sensual tension deepened and vibrated all around them. A strange lethargy seemed to grip her limbs, strange because even though it made her feel weak, it also made her pulses pound in mounting excitement.

She did want him so, she acknowledged to herself, swallowing thickly. How could she deny it if he tried to force the confession from her with these tactics?

"You look very good lying across my bed, your dark hair on my quilt," he said quietly. "I want you so badly, my little Leya, and I know you want me. I saw it in your eyes that first night in Oregon."

He shifted slightly, raising himself far enough to finish peeling off the shirt and hurling it to the floor. Then he reached down and slipped off his shoes, still anchoring her carefully.

One of Leya's evening sandals had already fallen silently to the floor beside the bed. Court pushed the other one off her foot and then stretched out along her length again.

"Court, please don't do this," Leya began, uttering each word with great care. She knew she was trembling now, and she also knew the reaction wasn't one of fear or anger.

He held her wrists in one hand above her head, letting his fingertips trail sensuously down the length of her throat.

"After tonight," he muttered, "you will play your games with no one else. I told you once in Oregon that I will be a very possessive lover, my sweet Leya. I meant it. I'm going to make sure that you know the limits of the golden chains . . ."

"Chains work both ways," she whispered, her nails curving into her palms. Instinctively, she lowered her lashes, watching his face through them. "The one who attaches a chain must continue to hold on to the other end. He is as much a prisoner as the one he would control."

"Do you think I don't know that?" Court growled, eyes blazing with a lambent flame. And then he was burying his lips in the scented place behind her ear.

Leya shivered again uncontrollably, and he abruptly released her hands, sensing her body's incipient capitulation with masculine certainty. Leya knew she was succumbing to the sensual power of the moment, knew she wanted him, perhaps even loved him. How did a woman resist the man she wanted when he let her know the full extent of his need as Court did now? How did a woman resist the man she was coming to love?

"Leya, Leya! Please don't deny me tonight," he begged. "Can't you see how I need you!"

She felt the passion in him as it mingled with her own, drawing them together in an elemental way that was nearly irresistible. It had been building throughout the evening, she knew, from the moment she had walked out of her bath to find him waiting for her.

He shifted, pulling her tightly against him so that he could find the zipper of her dress. She turned her face into his warm skin, inhaling the intoxicating maleness of him as he slipped the gown down over her shoulders. He lowered it slowly, tantalizingly, his lips following the receding barrier as sand birds follow the ebbing wave.

Tonight he did not tease her and tempt her with the seductive method he had used that last night in Oregon. Tonight Court set the pace, as if he wanted there to be no doubt this time about how it would end and no doubt about which of them was in final control.

"Oh, Court!" she breathed as his hand found her unprotected breast. She had worn no bra beneath the red-and-gold dress and he groaned softly as he claimed the treasure he sought. Her skin tingled as his fingers prompted forth the nipple, bringing it to a peak of hard desire that seemed to feed his own need.

"You could so easily drive a man over the edge, little Leya," he muttered as his lips burned a string of kisses up the curve of her throat. "All this passion combined with that damned independence! Harlow was a cretin to let you slip away from him. But I can't complain about his stupidity," he grated roughly. "It made things so much easier for me!"

"Easier!" she exclaimed huskily. "What do you mean? What would you have done if I had belonged to Alex by now?"

"Taken you away from him!" he declared savagely, and then his mouth closed hotly over hers, forcing apart her lips. His tongue swept inside just as his fingers tightened ever so slightly on the sensitive nipple. The combined attack sent a shiver roaring along Leya's spine, and she arched instinctively.

"But you would never have belonged to Alex," he rasped against her mouth a moment later as he broke the contact reluctantly. "You're much too smart for him. It would have been funny watching you handle him tonight if it hadn't been so infuriating watching you let him kiss you! I should punish you for that piece of impudence," he concluded on a thick groan as he lowered his mouth again.

Leya knew a surge of feminine triumph as she realized Court was far past the point of being able to punish her tonight. He was thoroughly caught up in the emotional turmoil seething around them, and the knowledge thrilled her. Deliberately, she allowed her fingers to wander down the line of his ribs to the hard waist.

He drew in his breath sharply when she unclasped his belt buckle and toyed with the opening of his slacks.

"Little wanton," he whispered on a husky note of laughter. "I knew you were a born tease the first day I met you! There's only one way to handle a tease." He pulled the dress lower, sliding it down over her hips and off completely.

"How do you handle a tease?" she challenged deep in her throat, loving the feel of his hands as he stripped off her pantyhose and left her in only the red lace bikini briefs.

"Make sure she plays the game out to the very end, of course. She'll learn her lesson!" He nipped her shoulder, letting her feel the edge of his teeth in a sharp caress that made her gasp.

Instantly, her trembling fingers clutched the skin of his hips, pushing aside the unbuckled slacks. Then she slid her palms up the sleek back, pausing to probe and explore as she headed for the fine hair at the back of his neck.

He moved, settling himself on his side and using his strong hands to tug her against him, letting her feel the rising need and the pounding of his heart.

"You're mine, Leya," he almost snarled as his fingers curved around her hips, dragging her against him. His lips haunted the region of her breast in deeper, more demanding kisses. "Admit it!" he commanded, and then his mouth fastened on her nipple. A second later she felt his tongue begin a delicate pattern and finally his teeth.

"Oh!" she moaned, her body enjoying the deliciously ravaging caresses beyond anything it had known in the past. "Oh, my God! Court! I want you so much!" The words were torn from her on a breathless cry as she wrapped her arms around his neck and clung.

"Enough to admit you belong to me?" he charged, his heavy thigh trapping her twisting, writhing legs. "Enough to admit that from now on no other man has a claim on you?"

She heard the passionate demand in his words and wondered at it.

"Answer me, Leya!" he gritted, pushing her onto her back and lowering himself roughly between her legs.

She felt the harshness of his slacks against the smoothness of her inner thighs and opened her eyes to find the melting gold and brown flaming over her face.

"I want you, Court," she whispered, her fingers gliding through the curling hair of his chest. "You are right about that," she confessed softly. "I've wanted you from the beginning."

It felt good to admit that much, she realized. It freed her somehow, made it possible to sink more deeply into the quicksand that was dragging at her, inviting her, overwhelming her . . .

"That's a start," he grated with a measure of satisfaction and relief in his voice as he slid passionately down her body, raining kisses over her breasts and on the soft skin of her gently curving stomach. "It's a beginning, at least."

Her hands locked in the thickness of his hair as he sank his teeth ever so carefully into the vulnerable flesh of her thigh.

Leya moaned and his hands held her still when she would have writhed against him.

"A start, Court?" she gasped. "What else would you have of me?"

"Everything!"

He began working his way back up her body. She could feel the rough texture of his slacks between her naked legs, knew the strength of his need as he arched himself intimately against her.

"Everything, my darling Leya," he continued more gently, curling a tongue around a taut nipple and cupping the breast with soft possession. "And I'll have it before this night is done. I must have it!"

She shuddered at the force of his demand and

wondered if she would be able to resist. Already she was unbelievably caught up in the maelstrom of his lovemaking. How much would she surrender before morning?

The power in him flowed over her, summoning forth a response Leya had never dreamed she was capable of generating. Her nails raking across his shoulders in small violent attacks seemed to excite him further.

His fingers feathered the inside of her thigh, the softness of her stomach, and the sensitive skin of her breast and throat. He touched her everywhere, as if he couldn't get enough of the feel of her.

At last, with impatient, wrenching movements, he stripped off the remainder of his clothes, lowering himself quickly back down beside her and pulling her into his arms.

"My God, Leya, I dreamed about this last night after I'd taken you home, do you know that?" he gritted, running exploring hands down to the ultra-sensitive area at the base of her spine. "I could see you here beside me, telling me that you wanted me, that you weren't going to punish me any longer for what had happened in Oregon . . ."

His fingers dug gently, intoxicatingly into the resilient flesh of her buttocks, and Leya gasped, her own hands gliding up his smoothly muscled chest. She bent her head, kissing the male nipples with a sensuous abandon.

"Oh, Court," she breathed again and again, wonder and chaotic emotion in her words as she contemplated what was happening.

"It's all right," he soothed passionately, stroking her back and pulling her ever closer. His mouth was hovering in her hair and he kissed the tip of her ear. "Tonight we start over, just as we agreed at the party. You won't regret it, Leya, I swear. This was meant to be. You've already admitted you want me. The rest will be easy . . ."

"Will it, Court?" she whispered, the words almost blocked in her throat.

"The only thing standing in our way was your need to avenge yourself; to get even for the way I had deceived you in Oregon. You did that tonight. I can't blame you, I've told you that. Hell, I would have done the same. We're a lot alike, you and I."

"You think you understand me so well," she murmured into the skin of his shoulder.

"Yes," he agreed unhesitatingly, twining his legs around her restless limbs and preparing to push her gently onto her back. "And very soon I will understand you even better. I will know exactly what drives you wild in my arms and what it takes to make you curl against me like a kitten. I will hear you tell me exactly how much you want me . . ."

"I want you."

"And need me . . ."

"I need you."

"And trust me . . ."

Leya went very still in his arms. He felt it instantly, and she lifted her lashes to find him staring down at her flushed features.

"Leya?" he growled almost harshly.

"What, Court?"

"Tell me you trust me. Admit that, just as you admitted that you wanted me and needed me!"

She felt the compelling urgency in him and blinked, confused. "Is it so important?"

"Yes, damn it! Tell me!"

She licked suddenly dry lips, aware of the violent tension in him and uncertain how to deal with it. "I want you, Court. Let that be enough for tonight."

"No, it's not enough!" he rasped, lifting his hands to tighten them fiercely around her shoulders. "I want to know everything!"

"Court!" His name was a helpless cry torn from her lips.

"Leya, please! This isn't a game!"

She was shaken by the intensity in every taut line of his face, unnerved by the tightness in him.

"I know it's not a game," she breathed. "That's why I can't give you what you ask. Let it be, Court. I want you, I've given you that much of a victory. Take it and have done!"

"You haven't forgiven me for what happened in Oregon, have you?" he snarled. "You aren't satisfied with your revenge."

"I'm not plotting revenge, Court," she gasped. "Not anymore. If I were, I wouldn't be here beside you, telling you that I want you and need you . . ."

"Leya, don't do this to me! To both of us!"

She was shocked at the words, and the knowledge that he was genuinely serious about his demand was almost therapeutic in its effect on her will. It was a therapy she could have done without, she thought sadly.

"Is that all you can think of, even now? Winning completely? Can't you take the compromise I'm offering? What's so important about having my trust? Or do you need that to assure yourself you've conquered the challenge completely?"

"Leya, you don't understand! I have to know you trust me. If you can't say the words, then I'll know you haven't yet satisfied your need for revenge. It's not a question of conquering a challenge, damn it. Can't you get that through your head? I know you needed to punish me, but you've done that. You can't keep doing it!"

"I'm not punishing you!" she hissed, beginning to push against his hard body. "You're asking more than I can give. Stop insisting on total victory, damn it. I thought that, if nothing else, we could at least go to bed together as equals, both of us admitting that we wanted each other. But you can't even compromise that much, can you? You can think only in terms of . . . of defeating me completely!"

With a final exclamation of male outrage, he gathered her flailing hands tightly in his fist and pushed her flat onto the bed. His eyes raked her softly gleaming body, lingering hungrily over the wantonly vulnerable curves.

"Look at me," he growled violently as she lay stretched out helplessly beneath him. "Look at me and try to guess just what a man could do to a soft little thing like you if he wanted to defeat you completely!"

He saw the hint of uncertain, bright-eyed fear coloring the silver green of her gaze and smiled savagely. "That's right, little shrew. A man who was intent on 'total victory,' as you call it, would have a very clearcut option open to him at this point, wouldn't he? Do you even realize just how helpless you are right now?"

He grasped the sable braid and pulled it significantly across her exposed throat. Leya trembled.

"Court! You wouldn't. You wouldn't rape me," she managed painfully, lying very still as her active imagination filled in the details. To be taken in rage and violence! The thought sickened her, repelled her, frightened her on the most primitive of levels.

"No," he agreed furiously, "I wouldn't. And something tells me that of the two of us, I'm the bigger fool!"

He wrenched himself away from her, his feet hitting the carpeted floor beside the bed with a thud. With swift, forceful motions, he threw on his clothes and tossed hers across her sprawled body.

"Get dressed," he grated. "I'm taking you home."

She watched him walk out of the room, trembling so badly she could hardly pick up her garments.

She found him pacing the floor in front of the fireplace when she finally emerged a few minutes later, some of her dignity and spirit mercifully restored along with her clothes. He looked up at once and halted, eyes shimmering with an enigmatic expression.

"I'll have to give you credit, Leya," he drawled as his gaze swept her from head to foot. "You have an instinct for good weapons."

"What are you talking about?" she muttered, coming forward slowly, warily.

"I expected to be punished for what happened in Oregon. It was inevitable you'd want revenge. I accepted that, thought I could deal with it and then put it all behind us. I talked myself into thinking I had convinced you that tonight's scene with Harlow constituted sufficient vengeance. But—"

"Will you stop talking like that?" she broke in

angrily, her hand moving in a gesture of denial. "I'm not plotting revenge!"

"No, I suppose you aren't. It came instinctively, didn't it? You seized the one weapon against which I don't have a defense. You've denied me your trust. How the hell am I supposed to fight that, Leya? How do I convince you you've punished me enough? How do I win back your trust, for God's sake?"

She stared at him in silence, aware of the ragged frustration in his words. He was absolutely right. Unwittingly, she had found a way to deny him his final victory.

"I don't know, Court," she whispered. "I don't know."

Chapter Eight

*R*evenge, Leya thought grimly the next morning as she dragged herself out of bed after an almost sleepless night. Was that what she was seeking by denying Court her trust? Was she doing it deliberately?

No, she told herself as she showered and dressed in a white skirt and multistriped blouse. It was nothing as simple and straightforward as that, regardless of what he thought. She had none of the satisfaction she'd had when she'd gotten even with Alex. There was none of the bubbling, cheerful amusement at seeing a foe vanquished. All she felt was depressed and unhappy. There was a strong wish that things could have been different between herself and Court; that things could have gone on the way they had started in Oregon.

But Oregon was behind her and reality was back. Leya clipped on turquoise earrings that matched one of the stripes in the blouse and headed downstairs to breakfast. There had been something very final about the way Court had driven her home in silence last night and left her at the door. Had he finally accepted the impossibility of continuing any relationship?

The renovated downtown mall area of Santa Rosa slumbered peacefully, waiting for the shopping day to begin as Leya parked her small, sassy little car in front of Brandon Books. As early as she was, it looked as if Cynthia was ahead of her. She glimpsed a figure moving about in the back of the shop as she slipped her key into the door.

"Hi, Cynthia," she called, shutting the door behind her. "It's only me, Leya."

"Leya! What are you doing here? You're supposed to be on vacation!"

Cynthia Dalton, the young black woman Leya had hired to help out part time, straightened from the box of new books she had been unpacking and smiled in welcoming surprise. She was an attractive person with an even more attractive personality and a liking for the book business.

Her close-cropped hair was cut with a touch of sophistication that emphasized the intelligent brown eyes and high cheekbones. This morning she wore the gold-hoop pierced earrings Leya had made for her as a birthday present earlier in the year and a stylishly casual pantsuit.

"I got back early from Oregon," Leya explained, not wanting to go into details. "But don't worry, I still want you to finish working full time this week. It will give us a chance to do some planning for that expansion into the shopping mall."

This job was important to Cynthia, who was working part time and taking college classes in business administration at night. Leya knew she had been happy to get in the extra hours at the bookstore when her boss had announced her sudden vacation plans.

"Couldn't stay away, hmmm?" Cynthia teased. "Well, don't worry. No major disasters around here. I thought I'd change the science fiction display today and finish unpacking this new shipment of romances. You know how many of our regulars will be pouring into the shop today looking for them."

Leya nodded, idly circling around behind the counter and picking up the latest copy of *Publishers Weekly*. She flipped through it absently, glancing at the announcements of new books.

"Been busy?"

"The usual daily crush. Nothing out of the ordinary. A lot of kids in the afternoons after school but they seem pretty well behaved. They're going wild over that new war game we put in the front window display."

Leya looked up and grinned in spite of herself. "We should declare a business holiday in honor of our brilliant decision to include war games and space-movie paraphernalia in our regular inventory. Do you realize that we've attracted a whole new crowd of customers? The people into that stuff are as much a breed of addict as the folks into mysteries, westerns, and romances! Bless their little hearts!"

Cynthia nodded in satisfaction, switching on the automatic drip coffeemaker on the little stand behind the counter. "There are worse habits in this world than books and games. We're doing humankind a favor the way I look at it!"

"And we're not doing too badly ourselves, either," Leya murmured, glancing thoughtfully around the well-organized shop. Unlike her home, the place was neatly arranged with easily identifiable categories. Mystery buffs knew exactly where to head the moment they arrived, as did the World War II history types and the science fiction fans.

The shop concentrated on paperbacks and, thanks in part to a good location, had been an immediate success almost from the start. The addition of the exciting and sophisticated space and war-games section had given it another boost.

The morning wore on, with Leya deliberately refusing to think about the previous evening. She buried herself in plans for the new branch of Brandon Books, going over sketches, estimating order quantities, and discussing hours of operation with Cynthia.

She was involved with a shelving plan, working at the back of the shop while Cynthia handled the customer traffic, when a shadow fell on the paper in front of her. She looked up to find Court standing beside the small table on which she was sketching. She started, not having heard him enter the shop.

"Hello, Leya," he said softly, but there was a cool wariness in the tortoiseshell eyes, instead of the masculine assurance that had always been there in the past.

"Hello, Court," she said carefully, wishing he wouldn't tower over her in such a fashion. He was dressed in a lightweight business suit, a single slash of color in his tie relieving the overall darkness of the outfit. Leya got to her feet in an automatic attempt to counteract the overwhelming sensation his presence provided.

"The woman at the counter said you were sitting back here," he told her by way of explanation. "I came to see if you will have lunch with me."

"Why?" The question came out stark and cold.

"Why do you think?" he retorted, a trace of impatience in his words now. "We have to talk."

"There's nothing to talk about, Court," Leya said wearily.

"The hell there isn't! Leya, you can't act as if nothing happened between us!"

"Will you please keep your voice down? I don't want the customers to hear you!"

"Then have lunch with me!"

"Or else you'll make a scene?" she mocked, her hands doubling into fists at her sides, her eyes defiant.

He ran a hand through his hair in clear exasperation. "I didn't come here to start a fight. I came to ask you to lunch. Please?"

She sensed the effort that had gone into the tacked-on plea and tilted her head slightly to one side, considering him. "Haven't you had enough from me, Court? I'm sorry if I couldn't satisfy your male ego completely, but . . ."

"Stop talking like that. Look, I want to get things back on a normal footing, Leya, for all our sakes."

"All? You're worried about my brother's reaction to our little, er, misunderstanding?" she asked tightly. "You're afraid I'll turn him against you and make your plans for Brandon Security more difficult to execute?"

"No!" he exploded and then obviously took a grip on himself. "Will you come with me, Leya?"

She met his eyes, saw the willpower he was using to keep from losing his patience, and realized there was something satisfying in that. He was making an effort, perhaps his first real effort to treat her as someone besides a woman he was arrogantly confident he could have.

"Sure, Court, I'll have lunch with you," she told him with sudden breeziness and smiled as he looked taken aback. "Just let me tell Cynthia where I'm going." Suddenly, she felt like the confident one.

He followed her down the aisles of books, his eyes roving over the shop's interior with undisguised curiosity.

"Cynthia, this is Court Tremayne. He works with my brother at Brandon Security."

Cynthia smiled warmly, and Court nodded politely, his eyes softening as he shook hands.

"You two are running quite a large operation here," he observed, glancing around again. "When Keith explained about the book business, I assumed it would be a much smaller affair."

"Bookstores have to be fairly large to be profitable," Cynthia explained, when Leya showed no signs of responding to the implied question. "The new one we're opening out in the mall is even bigger."

"Who will manage that branch?"

"I will," Cynthia smiled, slanting a curious glance at a silent Leya. "I'll have finished school by then and can work full time."

"Court is taking me to lunch, Cynthia. I'll be back in an hour, okay?"

"No problem. I brought a sandwich, as usual. Have a good time." Her dark eyes followed Court and Leya out of the shop, a speculative smile on her lips.

"There's a sandwich shop on the corner," Leya

began briskly as they stepped out onto the sidewalk. She started off without waiting for his nod of agreement, only to find her wrist lightly caught and held.

"I have a better idea," he said softly as she came to a stop and looked up at him inquiringly. "There's a nicer, more private place at the other end of the mall. I tried it once with your brother. We'll go there."

Leya hesitated knowing that for "private" she could read "intimate."

"All right, you're buying," she finally agreed flippantly.

Retaining his grip on her hand, Court started off in the other direction, his long strides forcing Leya to hurry.

"What is it you wanted to talk to me about, Court?"

"I'm impressed with the bookstore, Leya. You should be proud of having beaten the odds."

"What odds?" she frowned, disconcerted at the note of honest admiration in his voice.

"The odds against small-business success," he smiled, glancing down at her as they reached the restaurant. "You must have a real flair for the free-enterprise system."

"Is that why you came by today? To see if I really do know anything about business? To find out how much of a threat I might be to Brandon Security with my shares of stock?" she asked sweetly as they were shown to their table.

He shut his eyes, drew a long breath. "No. I meant what I said with no hidden meanings. I *am* impressed. A simple compliment from one businessperson to another. Take it or leave it."

She eyed him as she picked up the tasseled menu. He

was serious. Abruptly, Leya knew she was willing to help him with the truce.

"Okay, Court, I'll take it the way you say you mean it," she said calmly.

"Thanks," he muttered dryly, watching her smile as if he didn't quite trust it. "A glass of wine?"

"Fine."

They gave their orders and then the intimacy of the small booth closed in around them. Leya felt again the tension that never seemed absent when they were together, regardless of the circumstances.

"Now what did you really want to talk about, Court?" she finally asked softly, swirling the chilled chablis in her glass.

"You know very well what the subject is," he stated quietly, holding her eyes steadily. "We have to figure out where we're going from here."

"That's simple enough. Back to work. We both still have half a day left."

"Leya!"

"Okay, okay," she apologized, her fingers moving restlessly on the stem of the glass. "Suppose you tell me what you want from me. I was willing, too willing, to give much too much last night. If you've come to demand even more of me—"

"But I am, Leya," he interrupted tersely. "I want a lot more. Can't you understand that?"

"You don't let up, do you, Court?"

"Honey, listen to me! I'm not going to give up on what we had together in Oregon!"

"It's gone, Court."

"That's a lie! When I take you in my arms—"

"Please! Don't talk like that! You're embarrassing

162

me!" she gritted, flushing furiously. "This is a public restaurant!"

"I'm sorry, but you're making this so damn difficult," he muttered, swallowing a gulp of wine. The gold and brown of his eyes flowed over her intently, aggressively. "Can't you see what you're doing with this stupid plan of revenge? You're stringing me out on a rope that has no apparent end. If you picked a finite sort of punishment, something we could get over and done with, I could deal with it. But this business of telling me you no longer trust me . . ."

"What am I supposed to do? Tell you I'm willing to let bygones be bygones? Forget what happened and pretend I have no reason not to trust you?" she hissed wretchedly.

"Yes!"

"How?" she blazed.

"You could if you loved me," he whispered in a deep, dark growl, his eyes heating.

Leya froze, appalled. No! she wanted to scream at him. No! I don't love you. How could I possibly love you? But the words wouldn't come. They were blocked in her throat as she realized she didn't have the strength to say them.

"You ask too much, Court," she whispered stonily.

"Do I? More than you could have given if you had never learned about my deception? More than we would have had together if we were still in Oregon?"

"We'll never know, will we?" she countered tightly.

"Yes, damn it! We will know! I'll find a way if it kills me!"

"Why are you so upset about this?" she asked belligerently. "I'll give you my word not to interfere with Brandon Security. What's the matter? Don't you trust me, either?"

"How many times do I have to tell you this has nothing to do with Keith's business? This is strictly between us. Leya, give me a chance, damn it. Don't insist on throwing away everything we could have together just because you're angry at me. That's juvenile!"

"So now I'm being childish?" she retorted, arching one eyebrow quellingly. "You're not pleading your case very eloquently, Court. No woman likes to be told she's behaving in a juvenile fashion!"

"Even if it's the truth?" he shot back.

"Especially not then! But it's not the truth, is it? If I were really behaving like a foolish child, I would let you talk me into forgetting everything that happened. I'd let you give me a pair of rose-colored glasses. It's the adult in me that learns from mistakes, Court. It's the adult side of my nature that warns me to be so cautious about trusting strangers!"

"But you're implicitly demanding that I somehow prove myself before you'll agree to give me another chance! How does a man do that? There aren't any dragons out there waiting to be defeated in your name! There's nothing I can give you that would convince you you've misjudged me. Tell me what the hell I'm supposed to do!"

Leya blinked at the grimness of his tone, uncertain how to deal with him in this mood. He was angry, impatient, frustrated, and intent on changing her mind about him. She felt as if she were holding a powder keg.

"Trust is a fragile thing, Court," she began carefully. "It would take time—"

"How much time?" he interrupted at once, pouncing on the words.

"More time than you would probably be willing to spend on the project!"

"Tell me!"

"I don't know," she groaned, wondering how they had ever gotten into a bargaining situation like this. "I suppose we would have to get to know each other all over again . . ."

"No," he declared flatly. "But you could give me another chance," he countered at once, spearing a radish in his salad as if it were threatening to attack him.

"What's that supposed to mean?" she demanded warily.

"Exactly what it sounds like!"

"Court!"

"Have dinner with me tomorrow night at my place," he commanded intently, his eyes half-pleading, half-demanding. "Spend some time with me. Let me show you I'm still the man you were falling in love with in Oregon."

"Who said I was falling in love with you?" she demanded fiercely.

"The man you might have fallen in love with if I hadn't turned out to be such an unreliable bastard," he corrected wryly, holding up his fork placatingly. "Please, Leya?"

She hesitated. "Do you promise not to try and seduce me?" she muttered broodingly.

"No," he admitted at once, looking uncontrite.

"Then forget it!"

He sucked in his breath. "Leya, have dinner with me

and I'll promise not to force you into bed or anything else you don't want. That's as much a promise as I can give. Not that you need it," he went on in obvious irritation. "You can always use your ultimate weapon if things start getting too involved!"

"My lack of trust would be enough to stop you in another situation like last night?" Leya narrowed her eyes skeptically. He might have halted his lovemaking last night out of sheer annoyance at her unwillingness to grant him a complete victory, but that was certainly no guarantee he would do it again!

"You've known from the beginning I would never force myself on you," he told her with cold pride. "I didn't in Oregon when I probably should have and I won't do it here. At least give me that much of your trust!"

Leya stared at him, uneasily remembering that he was right. He could have pushed her into bed that night at the inn when she'd signed the contract. The electricity had been flowing heavily between them, and it wouldn't have taken much for him to overcome her defenses. That was nothing less than the truth, she acknowledged with painful honesty.

"All right, Court. I'll come to dinner at your apartment."

The corners of his mouth lifted in unexpected wry humor, and the familiar charm warmed his eyes. "The first step is always the hardest, sweetheart," he consoled her gently. "But I'll see you won't regret it."

Cynthia glanced up an hour later when Leya walked back into the shop, her dark eyes full of questions.

"Don't ask, Cynthia," Leya advised dryly. "I'm not sure I understand myself."

"He, uh, wouldn't by any chance be the reason you cut the Oregon vacation short, would he?" her friend asked perceptively.

"He is," she admitted grimly.

"I like him, Leya."

"I did too. For a while."

Cynthia was a good enough friend to know when not to press an issue like this one. Both women went back to their work without further discussion of the matter.

She hadn't really committed herself to anything, Leya assured herself the next day as she slipped a bottle of wine into a carrying bag and slid into the front seat of her car.

She was wearing a pair of straight-legged jeans with the cuffs rolled up to adjust the length. The dark sable braid lay across the breast of her cheerful yellow blouse, and a bright gold medallion glittered at the hollow of her throat.

No, there was no commitment involved in simply accepting Court's dinner invitation. And she wanted so much to be with him, she thought self-deprecatingly. She was willing to accept his patently false assurances because it gave her an excuse to agree to the date.

But she would make certain he abided by his own promises, Leya told herself staunchly as she parked the car in front of Court's rented condominium. She would not let him lure her here and then seduce her! If he truly wanted a genuine relationship, he could darn well work at it!

"Don't look at me as if I were Dracula inviting you into his castle!" were Court's first words when he opened the door to her that evening.

"Sorry," she murmured wryly, stepping inside and thrusting the wine toward him. "Do I look a tad cautious?"

"You look as if you're expecting me to close the door behind you and lock it," he grumbled, taking the wine and running a quick, appreciative eye over the label. "This looks terrific. Come on and I'll pour you a glass. Maybe it will relax you."

She followed him toward the kitchen, her eyes roving curiously over the dinner preparations. Two very thick steaks waited on a grill and a variety of lettuces had been torn into a glass bowl. A pile of scrubbed mushrooms waited in a frying pan.

"You really have nothing to fear tonight," he told her, deftly removing the cork and reaching for two long-stemmed glasses.

"No?"

"No. But I think you know that or you wouldn't have come. Admit you had to trust me a little in order to risk accepting the invitation this evening!" he challenged.

"Oh, I think you're busy regrouping your forces, trying to plan your strategy. I figure I'm safe enough until you decide how you're going to make your next move!" she told him with a deliberately teasing smile as she accepted the wine.

He caught the smile and his eyes returned it. "You're such a stubborn little thing," he sighed. "What am I going to have to do to make you stop fighting me?"

"Stop seeing me as a challenge," she retorted instantly. "Who knows what might happen if you simply saw me as a woman without any connection to Keith Brandon and Brandon Security?"

Court quietly helped himself to a hot pepper from the snack plate. He leaned back in the tan chair, relaxing visibly as if having gotten her this far he could afford to do so. He was wearing a khaki cotton shirt and close-fitting slacks. The masculine essence of him struck at her senses as it always did, making her fingers tingle to touch him.

"How can I ever make you believe I want you for purely personal reasons?" he asked a little grimly.

"I've never doubted your reasons were personal," she got out with a blitheness she was far from feeling.

He groaned and set down his wine glass with a small clatter. "I think we'd better find a more neutral topic." He got to his feet and reached for her hand. "Come here, Leya."

"Where are we going?"

"The bedroom," he told her with relish.

"The hell we are!"

"The *other* bedroom," he clarified, relenting. "You showed me something of yourself today and I mean to return the favor."

Curious, she allowed herself to be guided toward the second bedroom of the condominium. He threw open the door with an expectant glance down at her face.

"You asked me once what I did when I wasn't working. Well, this is part of what I do."

"A ham radio?" Leya walked forward and surveyed the sleek transceiver and related equipment arranged on a long table.

"I got into it when I was a kid and I've never managed to kick the habit," he confessed, watching her closely.

"I've always wondered what people talk about on these things," she said, turning to him with a quick smile. "I mean when they're not using them in emergency situations."

"I'm afraid the conversations tend to be fairly similar. The weather, radio equipment, and things like that. After all, the important thing is making the contact. I've talked to people in Japan and Eastern Europe. There's something fascinating about communicating with other hams so far away."

"Fascinating? Or challenging?"

"Leya, my sweet, if you're not awfully careful I'm going to withhold your steak tonight and feed you hamburger, instead!"

"I'll behave!" she promised instantly, laughing up at him as she lifted the stack of QSL cards and started flipping through them. "What are these?"

"Cards from people I've talked to documenting the contact. When I get the card, I enter each communication in that logbook over there."

"Well, I must admit, I prefer the idea of you industriously bent over your radio in the evenings to the picture of you industriously bent over a blonde!" she teased lightly, setting down the stack of cards.

"Meaning you wouldn't be jealous of the ham radio?" he inquired interestedly.

"If you're trying to make me admit I'd be jealous over the blondes . . ."

"No," he said quickly, brushing aside the statement. "I'm serious about the radio."

She frowned, not understanding. "Why on earth would anyone be jealous over a radio?"

"You'd be surprised," he said dryly.

"You spend a lot of time talking to *blondes* over the radio?" she taunted.

"Of course not. But I have been known to spend a lot of time on the equipment itself. Sometimes when I get started I can't walk away from it for hours. I've found that women aren't always so understanding about that kind of, er, involvement."

Leya laughed with sudden comprehension. "Sounds like me in my jewelry shop. Once I get going, I often can't quit until the current project is finished."

"Somehow," he said softly, "I had a feeling you'd understand."

Their eyes met in a curiously charged moment of mutual perception and strange recognition. Leya felt the tension around them and had to force herself to break it before it grew to dangerous proportions.

"I'm getting hungry," she said lightly, moving toward the door.

He stepped back to let her pass. "What a coincidence. So am I." He turned on his heel. "Let's get those steaks ready."

As if those few moments in the "ham shack" had initiated a truce both wanted to maintain, the conversation during dinner slipped back into the easy camaraderie that had existed in Oregon. In its own way, Leya realized belatedly, it was every bit as seductive as Court's outright lovemaking.

"How are you finding things at Brandon Security?" she asked politely, helping to clear the table and stack dishes in the sink. Neither suggested being so rash as to actually wash the plates and utensils.

"Challenging," Court retorted dryly, grinning at her as he carried in the last of the dishes from the dining-room table.

"I think I'm going to learn to hate that word," Leya complained, wiping her hands on a towel.

"Join the crowd," he invited succinctly.

"Seriously, Court, are things very bad?"

"You mean with the company or with me?"

"Court!"

"Okay," he said placatingly, his eyes laughing at her. "No, things aren't that disastrous, but there's going to be a hell of a lot of work involved during the next two years. Your father hadn't kept the manufacturing line updated."

"I thought he had started pouring a lot of money into that. There certainly wasn't much left when he died except the business."

"He'd made a start but a lot more needs to be done. And the research and development end of things has also gone downhill. It's a competitive market, security devices; a viable company has to consider research as important as manufacturing and marketing. The sales staff looks fairly decent, and your brother's commitment is total. Given that, things will work out, but it will take some basic reorganization and some rough priority setting."

"And the hope that the crime situation stays sufficiently unpleasant in the United States to produce a strong consumer demand for Brandon's products," Leya remarked wryly.

"Unfortunately, there doesn't appear to be any

danger of a lessening in demand. One of the first things I'm going to do when I move into your house is harden it."

"Who says you're going to be moving in!" Leya exclaimed, whirling to confront him. "And what do you mean by hardening it?"

"Sorry, slip of the tongue," he apologized meekly while Leya glared at him suspiciously. "As for hardening it, I meant make it more secure. The locks on your doors and windows would be child's play to someone seriously interested in entering illegally."

"You mean as you did that day you were waiting for me when I came out of the bathroom?" she reminded him irritably as they ambled into the living room and settled with equal lethargy back into their chairs.

"I didn't consider that a case of illegal entry," he murmured coolly, the gold in his eyes shimmering with memory. "I was coming to pick you up for a date, as I recall."

"This conversation is turning unsubtle. I can always tell when your patience is wearing thin, Court. You start losing your subtle approach," Leya declared, frowning into the fire, her arms resting along the curving back of the chair.

"That's a pity," he drawled, watching her profile. "I meant tonight to be very subtle, indeed. Why don't you come over here and let me show you?"

She turned her head at the wistful tone in his words and met his eyes.

"Show me what, Court?" she breathed, feeling the sensual tug of unseen golden chains.

"How subtle I can be," he replied softly, eyes warming with a heat that communicated itself to her.

He didn't move, but it was as if he were reaching out to her, drawing on the ends of the chains. "Remember how it was in Oregon, honey? No force, no demands except the ones you, yourself, create. You have my word. I won't even come and get you. I'll let you do everything on your own."

Chapter Nine

$\mathcal{U}$nable to deny the restlessness his words and eyes elicited, Leya got to her feet, resolutely crossing to the fire. She didn't hear him get to his feet behind her, but she knew he was there, only inches away. He could have put his hands around her waist and drawn her back against him, but he didn't.

"Do you know how badly I want to make love to you, Leya?" he asked in a voice that had turned faintly raspy with desire.

She felt the flutter along her spine and stood very still, her eyes focused on the flames in front of her. "I thought you wanted the words first, Court. I thought you wanted to know how much I *trust* you," she said quite distinctly, knowing that if he put out his hand she would tremble beneath the touch. He probably knew it, too. Every time he touched her, she seemed to have less and less resistance, Leya thought dazedly.

"Can't you give me the words, Leya?" he begged a little thickly, lowering his head to drop the tiniest of shivering kisses on the back of her neck.

Leya flinched, as she had known she would, but she couldn't bring herself to step away from the implicit danger.

"And hand you your victory on a silver platter?" she asked, sensing his arousal and the control he was exerting over himself. It touched a chord of excitement deep in her body, emboldened her in some strange fashion.

"It's not a question of victory or challenge," he whispered, once again touching his lips to her nape. She knew he must have sensed her inner tremor. "When you realize that, you'll realize you're only hurting both of us by being so stubborn."

His hands went to her waist, settling there lightly, with no compulsion. Slowly, she turned within the circle of the embrace and met his eyes with a searching gaze.

"Am I hurting you, Court?"

"You're driving me crazy!" he gritted before taking her lips in the most feather-light of kisses. "And, yes, it hurts!"

Of their own accord, Leya's arms wrapped themselves around his neck, her body urging a closer contact with this man who could inflame her senses so easily. It would be safe tonight, she told herself silently. He wouldn't dare risk forcing her beyond the limits she wanted to set. He wouldn't want to jeopardize the future victory. Would he?

But he was leading her on again, his mouth persuasive, coaxing, cajoling, but not demanding. As she had the night at the inn, Leya felt herself responding to the safe lovemaking he seemed to promise.

Her body inclined toward his and she felt his hands slide down the length of her spine, seeking the intimate feel of her. He stood braced, his feet slightly apart and gently urged her hips against his lower body, inviting her into his warmth.

She groaned against his mouth and parted her lips, luring him into the sensual investigation he sought.

"Leya!"

Her name was a husky whisper as she moved against him and his hands tightened perceptibly. She moved her head, seeking the tanned column of his throat and felt him tremble as she scorched kisses down to the opening of his khaki shirt.

She loved this, she realized dimly. She loved the feel of him, she loved making love to him. She loved his response . . .

"You really are intending to drive me crazy, aren't you?" he growled, his fingers digging erotically into the curve of her derrière.

"And if I am?" she taunted, alive with the scent and feel of him.

"I'll just have to endure the punishment, won't I?" he mocked gently.

He moved, taking a step backward and sinking into the sofa, pulling her into a gentle sprawl on top of him.

She met his eyes, saw the deep male need there and responded to it. Slowly, she bent her head and kissed him, drawing out the teasing, provocative caress until she felt him shudder beneath her.

His hands held her more tightly against him, his legs stretched out so that she lay between them. Her own inner urgency grew as she began to explore the warm skin that disappeared beneath the collar of his shirt, and she was so engrossed with undoing the first button she encountered that she was hardly aware of it when his hands slid under the material of her yellow blouse.

Then, quite suddenly, his fingers were circling her breasts, seeking the sensitized nipples, and she knew he had undone the clasp of her bra. The electric shock of his touch brought her temporarily back to reality.

"Court, I don't—"

"Hush, Leya," he breathed, his fingers sliding under the small, full weight of her breasts while his thumbs probed the tips. "This is the way it was meant to be between us. We've both known that from the beginning."

"Court, I won't let you push me into bed!" she cried softly, almost beseechingly.

"Are you sure about that?" he half-smiled, some of his natural arrogance seeping through to alarm her.

"Some victory that would be!" she taunted desperately, knowing the precariousness of her situation now.

"What makes you think you'd be unwilling?" he charged roughly, eyes glittering as he raked her features. His fingers moved again on her breasts, and when she trembled in response, satisfaction flared in his gaze.

"You might succeed in forcing a response," she conceded, knowing it was useless to protest that fact. "But that wouldn't give you the victory you'd have if I were to admit I trusted you again, would it? I think you like your challenges completely conquered, Court Tremayne, not just partially!"

Something dangerous flickered through him, communicating itself to her body, and she suddenly sensed the deep masculine instinct that wanted to have done with the taunts and defiance.

"For a woman who's intent on not offering me a challenge, you seem very good at throwing down the gauntlet," he finally rasped warningly. "What would you do if I chose to pick it up?"

His hands closed like steel bands around her waist, holding her immobile.

"What are you talking about?" she demanded, feeling the prickle of fear.

"What if I decided not to wait for the words and simply took what was offered? And it was offered, Leya," he reminded her with a touch of savagery. "Last night you were more than willing! Perhaps I should have carried matters a little farther. Another few minutes and you might have been willing to say anything I wanted you to say!"

"Well, I certainly didn't have to worry about that happening, did I?" she flung back, incensed. "You made it very clear that the only way you want me is the way most flattering to your ego! You were in a rage last night when you drove me home. I think you would have cheerfully thrown me out the door if you hadn't felt somehow obliged to take me back home!"

"Did that bother you, sweetheart?" he breathed, some of the impatience in him fading. "Did it hurt *your* ego to know I could call a halt, get dressed, and take you home?"

"I don't know what dazzling conclusion you think

you've reached about my behavior," she began furiously, not liking the direction the conversation was taking.

"Did you think last night was easy on me?" he soothed, reaching up to toy with her dark braid as he smiled with affectionate amusement. "Don't you know how hard it was to take you home last night? Don't you know how I spent the remainder of the night staring at the ceiling of my room and thinking about how good you had felt in my arms? About the softness of your breasts and the way your nipples flower under my fingers like buds bursting into bloom? Don't you think I was in misery remembering the invitation in your eyes, the feel of your legs alongside mine?"

"Court!" she squeaked, turning several deepening shades of red at his totally unexpected verbal lovemaking. His eyes poured gold over her.

"Oh, I suffered last night, if that's what's worrying you," he assured her softly. "I wanted very badly to slip golden chains around you and listen to you make the sweet sounds of love."

"But you didn't want me badly enough to take me on my terms. You wanted a full surrender first!" she retorted accusingly.

"Maybe," he husked, cupping her face between rough palms and pulling her head down to his. "Maybe I do want to feel more certain of you. Is that so very strange?"

"Feeling certain of someone is not the same thing as . . . as demanding a complete surrender!"

"In our case," he said quite steadily as he dragged her mouth down onto his, "I think it might be!"

He swamped her now with the force of his passion,

unleashing all the uncompromising desire he had been holding in check. She felt the rising need in him and wanted to cry out. But her lips were captive to his.

He shifted his weight with a strong movement that reversed their positions on the sofa. In an instant he was covering her, letting her know the full weight of him as he began undoing the buttons of the yellow blouse.

"Court, no!"

"What's the matter, Leya?" he murmured into her throat as his hands once more claimed her breasts. "You have no need to fight me this time. I won't demand a confession of undying love and trust from you tonight!"

Pushing aside the fabric of the blouse, he bent his head to curl his tongue around the peak of her breast. Leya shuddered, her hands clenching in the thickness of his hair.

"Please! I don't want us to . . ."

"Last night you wanted it. You'll want it again tonight," he vowed.

She tried to move her legs, only to have him take advantage of the action and thrust his own between hers. Her senses spun.

"Oh!"

He ignored the small cry, his fingers sliding down the material of her jeans to find her hips in an urgent caress. She felt his tongue dip enticingly into her navel and her body arched upward instinctively.

"At least you can't hide your physical response!" he groaned, letting her feel his teeth on the softness of her stomach in an exquisite touch.

His fingers trailed down to play with the back of her

knee, massaging it through the jeans in an amazingly erotic movement that brought small moans from Leya's throat. Her hands glided down onto the muscles of his shoulders, and she dug in her nails with catlike intensity.

"Oh, my God, Court! Please!"

"Please, what, Leya?" he challenged, edging slowly back along the length of her body. "Please make love to you? I will. And I won't make the mistake I made last night."

"What mistake?" she demanded hoarsely, delighting in the feel of him as she pushed her hands under his shirt and clung to his strong back.

"I won't make any demands you're not prepared to satisfy," he swore. "We'll try it your way!"

"My way? I don't understand! What are you saying?"

She didn't want to think, but some restless part of her mind kept forcing her to do so. Something was wrong. She had to get a grip on the situation and herself. She *had* to! Already his fingers were undoing the snap of her jeans.

"Stop it, Court! What do you mean you won't make any demands? That's exactly what you're doing!"

"No, I'm not. I haven't asked anything of you yet," he said tersely, his fingers gripping the waistband of her jeans as he prepared to drag them down over her hips. "I haven't made you swear your trust or your faith in me or your undying love . . ."

Leya began to panic, realizing he was intent on pursuing the sexual goal without any of the words that would make it right. She twisted, struggling to loosen his grip, but he leaned the full weight of his body against her.

"What's the matter, Leya?" he rasped, raising his head to meet her now frantic gaze. "This was the way you wanted it last night, remember?"

"No! Not this way! You don't understand!"

"What don't I understand? You didn't want the words. All right, I agree to accept your terms!"

She heard the thread of harshness in his voice, felt it in the way he was handling her, and wanted to cry. Desperately, she pushed against his shoulders.

"Please," she begged, her lips trembling as she watched him, wide-eyed and terribly uncertain. "I don't want you to do this to me. Please, Court!"

"What do you want, Leya?" he demanded tightly, his hands stilling on her hips. "I'm trying to do this your way. Tell me what you want!"

"Damn you! Stop pushing me like this!" she wailed, doubling her hands into fists against the muscles of his shoulders. "I know what you're trying to do! You're trying to force me into a corner where I'll admit anything you want!"

"How can a man force a woman to say she trusts him?" he taunted bitterly.

"By pushing her to the point where she will say the words he wants rather than go through with the lovemaking without them!" Leya stormed furiously.

For a stark second, a curious silence hovered in the air. Then Court spoke very softly.

"Why should the words matter? Why can't you go through with the physical side of things without them? You were willing last night . . ."

"Last night—last night I was wrong," Leya returned in a heavy, unhappy whisper. "Last night I hoped . . ."

"What did you hope, Leya?" he prodded.

"Nothing," she said dismally. How could she explain that last night she had somehow hoped making love together might put things right between them? It was the kind of illusion women had tempted themselves with forever. And it was just as false now as it had been thousands of years ago. It took the words to make it right. The words of genuine commitment.

"You hoped that we would say all the right things to each other in the throes of passion?" he hazarded roughly.

"Yes!" she admitted with a hint of arrogant defiance. She would not let this man crush her spirit tonight!

His eyes blazed into hers for a long, unwavering moment, and then, so quickly that it startled her, he sat up, swinging his legs to the floor. His hand continued to rest on her vulnerable, naked stomach.

He turned his head to meet her questioning gaze. "Does it strike you," he began dryly, "that we think along the same lines? Now, all we have to do is get the timing coordinated!"

She edged carefully out from under his absently possessive hand, pulling her blouse around her and beginning to button it with unsteady fingers.

"You mean last night you wanted the words before the sex and tonight I wanted them," she agreed flatly, not looking at him.

"Tonight, I was the one who talked himself into thinking they could be put off until later," Court said gently, putting out a hand to touch her dark braid. "With any luck, maybe we've both learned something."

She glanced up sharply and found the gold of his eyes warming her intently.

"Court . . ."

"Come on, Leya," he ordered gently, getting to his feet. "It's time you went home."

She lay awake in bed a long time that night, thinking. Trust. It lay at the bottom of the issue. There was no denying the physical attraction between herself and Court. Instinctively, she knew that scenes such as the one she had just been through and the one the previous evening could repeat themselves indefinitely until one or the other of them succumbed to the lure of satisfaction without commitment and understanding.

But was the commitment Court wanted from her the same as the one she wanted from him? She had trusted Alex Harlow once and suffered the humiliation of being used. Court Tremayne was the only other man to have gained her trust to such an extent. And once again she had played the fool for a man.

Or had she? Court could have taken her tonight. Why hadn't he? Was it really so important to him that she commit herself fully? Did he need her trust because he needed *her?*

Deliberately, coldly, Leya applied the calculating, analytical portion of her mind to the enormous problem with which she was confronted. The pattern of moonlight on the ceiling shifted several times before she began to see a solution in it.

She needed to dissociate herself from Brandon

Security in Court Tremayne's mind, she finally realized. She needed to find out how long his interest in her would last if she were no longer connected with the business. Perhaps then they could truly start from scratch.

But what would she do if she took the step of severing all ties with Brandon and then found out Court lost interest in her?

Leya closed her eyes briefly against the potential misery and then firmed her resolve. There was no other way to clear the cluttered path between herself and Court. If they were to have another chance, she must take the one step to create the opportunity.

"I'm going to have to run over to Brandon Security and see my brother this morning, Cynthia," Leya announced the next day when she walked into the shop. "Will you mind holding the fort alone for a while?"

"Nope. I was prepared to do it all this week, anyhow, remember?" Cynthia chuckled, handing her boss a cup of coffee.

"He should be at work in another half-hour," Leya noted, accepting the coffee gratefully and perching herself on one of the tall stools behind the counter. She smoothed the denim skirt she was wearing with a red-and-white checked blouse and smiled wryly. "I've stopped dropping by his apartment unexpectedly in the early mornings!"

"You mean after the door was opened a few times by various females?" Cynthia laughed knowingly.

"Why are they always blonde, Cynthia?" Leya complained, thinking of her conversation on the subject with Court the night of the party. "And they all seem to look alike, too. I'm not sure how my brother tells them apart. Something about the eyes always looks the same!"

"Your brother is a smart man," Cynthia assured her sympathetically. "When it comes time to get serious, he'll pick one he can talk to out of bed as well as in it!"

"I hope so!"

They chatted a few minutes longer over coffee, and then Leya glanced at her watch. "I'd better be on my way if I'm going to catch Keith before he gets involved in a meeting or something. You've got the number if you need me."

"Right. Don't worry about this place. I'll call if anything goes wrong."

"It won't. I just like to have the illusion that I'm useful once in a while," Leya grinned, heading out the door.

But the grin disappeared as she slid into the front seat of her car. The stop at Brandon Books had been a delaying action and she knew it. The real business of the day lay ahead of her, and there was no sense putting it off any longer.

With a feeling that she was deliberately concocting her own doom, Leya pulled out into the early morning traffic and headed for the offices of Brandon Security Systems.

Several minutes later, she walked past a secretary's desk with a smiling nod and entered her brother's sanctum. She still experienced a pang on occasion when she did it, remembering how her father had once occupied the office. But the sadness didn't last long anymore. Keith had made the place his own in the months since he had moved in, and once inside, Leya was no longer disturbed by memories.

"'Morning, Leya, what's up?" Keith asked cheerfully, closing a folder he had been scanning. "Enjoying yourself with my new consultant?"

"Funny you should mention that," Leya began dryly.

"Uh-oh. I have a feeling Court should be here to handle this."

Keith eyed his sister warily. Smart younger brothers usually learned to assess a sister's moods early in life, Leya reflected wryly. And Keith was, as Cynthia had noted, smart.

"Not at all," she told him far too smoothly, dropping into a nearby chair. "This is between you and me, brother dear."

"The last time you called me 'brother dear' you wanted to borrow my motorcycle," Keith said reminiscently. "It was returned with a crumpled wheel."

"Dangerous things, motorcycles," Leya murmured sympathetically. "I'm glad you've had the sense not to buy another one."

"I've, uh, developed other interests."

"So I've noticed. But I'm not here to borrow anything today," Leya went on briskly, crossing one knee gracefully over the other and swinging her toe idly.

"You're here to chew me out for not having come to your rescue the other night when Court carried you off over his shoulder?" he hazarded, lifting one eyebrow.

"No, although an impartial observer might think I had cause to do so," she retorted, silver-green eyes glinting dangerously.

"Most impartial observers would have the sense to realize it doesn't pay to interfere in an argument of a domestic nature," Keith shot back easily, lounging into his chair. "Are you sure I shouldn't call Court in here? He's on a tour of the manufacturing facilities at the moment, but I can have him paged." Keith waited hopefully.

"I've told you this is between us, Keith."

"Okay, let's have it," he sighed in obvious resignation. "What do you want from me?"

"Nothing at all. I'm here to give you something." Leya fixed him with a cool, calculating glance.

"What?" He didn't look anxious to receive any gifts, she decided, smiling inwardly. A smart younger brother.

"My shares in Brandon Security Systems."

"Your what?" he demanded in stunned amazement. "Why the devil would you want to do that?" Keith leaned forward, resting his elbows on the wide mahogany desk, his green eyes staring at her.

"You know I've never had any real interest in the firm."

"Yes, but . . ."

"And now that you've hired yourself a man of great expertise to assist you in getting the company back on its feet, you don't need my 'silent' input any longer!" The hint of sarcasm was barely concealed.

"But this is part of your inheritance from Dad, Leya!"

"I don't want it or need it. You're the one who's taken to the business like a natural, Keith. There's no reason you shouldn't have it all."

"But Dad wanted you to have something!" he protested, waving a hand helplessly.

"He gave me my start in the book business, remember?"

"That was a loan, which you paid back!"

"Interest free," she reminded him with a smile. "And he gave it to me at a time when none of the banks would have touched me with a ten-foot pole. Besides, there was the money from the sale of the house, which you and I split. Believe me, Keith, I'm more than content with my inheritance."

Her brother eyed her thoughtfully, absently tapping the tip of a pencil on his desk. "This has something to do with your relationship with Court, doesn't it?"

"How did you guess?" she mocked grimly. "It may very well put an end to that relationship."

"But you're hoping it won't?"

"That's my business, Keith. Do I ask you pointed questions about all those blondes?"

"Yes!"

"Liar. I haven't asked any for ages!" she argued.

"Leya, I don't know what you're up to, but . . ."

"Don't worry, Keith, I know what I'm doing. And I truly don't want the shares in Brandon Security. I should have turned them over to you months ago," she added sincerely. She reached into the thin leather case at her side. "I've brought the papers with me. We should be able to take care of everything today."

"Are you certain this is what you want, Leya?" Keith asked slowly, scanning her face a few minutes later as they concluded the business.

"Yes, but there is one other small item," she drawled.

"I knew it!" he gritted with morbid satisfaction.

"I want you to make it very clear to Courtland Gannon Tremayne that there is no longer any gain to be had in remaining 'interested' in me," Leya said decisively, even as the raw pain of what she was doing cut deep.

"So that's it," Keith breathed, nodding his head finally in understanding. "You're an idiot, Leya. The man wants to marry you."

She flinched. "He's certainly never said anything about marriage to me!"

"Knowing you, you haven't given him a chance! You're probably still mad at him for deceiving you up there in Oregon!"

"He told you about that?" she asked disbelievingly.

"Yes, he did, and I think you're a fool to hold it against him!"

"Would you trust someone after he'd done something like that?" she hissed angrily.

"Depends on the someone. I'd trust Court," Keith declared forcefully.

"You've got a bad case of hero worship!" she accused, getting to her feet and starting for the door. Her glance halted at the bare spot on the opposite wall. "What did you do with my picture?" she turned back to ask curiously.

"Court asked me for it," Keith said briefly, watching

her expression with great interest. "He's got it hanging in his own office now."

"He does?" Leya swallowed her surprise.

"Ummm. I suppose he enjoys having an image of his *victim* handy to gloat over!" Keith retorted nastily.

Leya slammed out of the office.

Chapter Ten

$\mathcal{T}$he ringing of the doorbell shortly after Leya had returned home from work was not entirely unexpected. Court was not a coward. With a distinct feeling of impending disaster, Leya uncoiled herself from the couch and made her way toward the door.

Court stood on the threshold, still dressed in a business suit and dark tie, his gold-and-brown hair damp from a faint sprinkling of rain. The tortoiseshell eyes gleamed.

"Good evening, Leya," he said politely, propping himself against the edge of the door with one large hand. "I understand you've had a busy day."

"I merely took care of some business matters," she retorted loftily, her heart pounding with a strange hope. Was he here to mock her or woo her?

"So I gather. Get your jacket, I'm taking you out to dinner."

At the note of command in his voice, she stiffened. "I'm not very hungry."

"Then I'll force-feed you. I'm taking you out to eat, Leya, and to discuss our future. Don't bother fighting it, I'm not in a mood for your stubbornness this evening."

"What's the matter? Can't you say what you want to say right here? It shouldn't take long!" She faced him bravely.

"I'll give you the same choice I gave you the night of the party," he said politely. "You can come out on my arm or over my shoulder."

Leya drew herself up to her full height and fixed him with an angry glare. Why couldn't he get it over with right now? What was the point in dragging everything out? Either he was still interested or he wasn't. It should be so damned simple!

"Very well," she announced disdainfully, "if you're going to be that way about it!"

"I am," he assured her, but there was a slight smile in his eyes.

Leya didn't volunteer a word during the short drive to a nearby steak house, and Court didn't bother to open the conversation until after he'd ushered her into the darkened lounge and ordered both of them a drink.

"I needed that," he muttered thankfully a few minutes later as he took a swallow of the scotch and settled into the chair. His jacket had been removed and slung over the back, and he'd loosened his tie. He looked like any other businessman relaxing after a hard day at the office, Leya thought fleetingly, stifling an urge to touch his sleeve soothingly.

"Sleep well last night?" he inquired pleasantly.

"Don't be ridiculous," she responded tightly.

"Neither did I. I gather you spent the hours lying awake staring at your ceiling in useful contemplation, however," he went on blandly.

"You've talked to Keith?" she said as coolly as possible, her fingers curling around the cold glass in her hand.

"This afternoon. So you finally decided to turn your shares in Brandon Security over to your brother, hmmm? Should have done it long ago."

"It would have made everything so much *simpler*, wouldn't it?"

"Much!" He lifted his glass for another swallow.

"And you're a great one for taking the easiest path to a goal!" she went on sarcastically, sipping moodily at her drink.

"I try," he agreed modestly, watching her from beneath lowered lids. "But even I have to stand back in admiration of your talents along that line."

She eyed him sharply. "Meaning?"

"Meaning you very neatly removed the one obstacle I was powerless to remove. If I'd asked you to give up your shares in Brandon Security, you would have been certain I was determined to get you out of the picture."

"And now I've done it for you," she concluded morosely.

"Why?" he asked quietly.

She moved a hand in a small gesture that conveyed her inability to fully explain. "I . . . I wanted you to stop seeing me as an obstacle you had to overcome in order to have control at Brandon Security."

"I wonder how long it will take you to realize the full implications of what you did when you abdicated your rights at Brandon," he mused thoughtfully.

She frowned, bewildered.

"Don't you realize how much trust you demonstrated, sweetheart?" he said with a hint of a smile.

"I did no such thing! I merely decided to opt out of the stupid game we were playing!" she protested righteously.

"And leave your little brother to my mercy?" he murmured.

"What's wrong with that? You're going to . . . Oh!"

"Precisely. When did you stop worrying about my having designs on Brandon Security? When did you decide I would honor the spirit of the contract and not take advantage of Keith?"

She glanced away, her teeth sinking into her bottom lip briefly.

"Now it really is just between you and me," he went on softly. "You very graciously removed the one factor which was unduly complicating things, leaving us free to get on with this nutty relationship!"

"Is it still the 'challenge' thing, Court? Do you still have to take me to bed to prove something to yourself? There's nothing left to win! I removed the prize when I gave the shares to my brother. The game is over."

"The game isn't over until you admit you belong to me!" he gritted, his hand tightening vengefully around his glass as his temper clearly frayed. "And you *do* belong to me, Leya Brandon. I've seen it in those silver-green eyes since the first night I took you in my arms on the dance floor! The problem all along has been to get you to admit it!"

"You're so damn sure of yourself!" she snapped in sudden fury.

"I'm staking my hope of future peace of mind on the fact that you're going to belong to me, yes!"

"You'd like that, wouldn't you? It would satisfy that monstrous ego of yours to have me admit that!"

"It would certainly go a long way toward soothing it," he agreed bleakly, obviously making an effort to rein in his impatience. There were grimly etched lines around his mouth, and the determination in him was palpable.

You could tell just by looking at the man that he never gave up once he'd accepted a challenge, Leya thought miserably. She should have known giving away the stock wouldn't solve everything. No, she decided, something had changed.

He'd decided he wanted her and he was going to have her. But at least he wanted her now for herself, not as a way to buy himself into Brandon Security!

"If you thought I was prepared to throw myself into your bed the moment you showed any interest in me after I'd given away the stock, you were on the wrong track," she told him bitterly. But at least she was no longer a challenge directly connected with Brandon Security!

"For a couple of basically intelligent people, we're having a lot of trouble lately with words, aren't we?" he shot back.

"What do you suggest?"

"I suggest," he told her with sudden gentleness, his eyes gleaming, "that you let me make everything much easier for you."

"How?" she began suspiciously. "I'm not going to go to bed with you in an attempt to 'communicate'!"

"I've known all along that part of the problem is your pride," he said soothingly. "I've known it because you're a lot like me. Given the same set of circumstances, I'd have had a few problems along that line myself."

Leya felt like a pet rabbit being stroked by a wolf. "Very generous of you," she told him dryly.

"But I think you were trying to accomplish something important today by giving your stock to Keith. I think you were asking me to show you that my interest in you extends beyond the business. And I'm quite prepared to do that."

"You're going to be understanding about my pride problem?" she mocked warily.

"Definitely." He smiled, eyes crinkling beguilingly. "I've got a way to get around all the words."

"Ah! You're going to try and get me into bed without them after all!" she nodded wisely.

"It may come to that, but I'm going to try something else first."

Leya licked her lower lip with a short, quick stab of her tongue as she considered him cautiously. "Now what are you up to, Court Tremayne?"

"Intrigued, are you?" he chuckled, half-turning in his chair to dig into a coat pocket. "That gives me a decided advantage, you realize."

He removed a small jeweler's box from his coat and swiveled back around to face her. The green velvet box rested on the palm of his hand as he held it out to her.

"A ring?" she asked disbelievingly, her untrusting eyes going from the proffered gift to his glittering gaze.

"No, not a ring. A ring is easy to slip on and off. In

our case this will represent a more binding commitment, I think." He made no move to force the gift into her hand, merely holding it out to her with a waiting quality in his expression.

The atmosphere grew very still and dangerous. Leya couldn't take her eyes off the small green box, in spite of the sensation of menace. He was right. She was intrigued now. Not a ring? Of course not. That would have been too much to hope for. Court wasn't asking her to marry him.

"Come on, Leya," he coaxed on a note of amusement. "Take a risk."

She frowned and reached out to pluck the box from his hand. Her imagination was working overtime, she chided herself. There was no danger here.

"Open it," he prodded gently.

Surprised at the degree of boldness it took, Leya snapped open the green velvet lid and gave a small exclamation at the beautifully worked emerald earrings inside. Her knowledgeable eye admired the delicate craftsmanship and the quality of the stones before she had a chance to really think about it.

"They're . . . they're lovely, Court," she finally managed, a trifle breathlessly. "But I can't accept a gift like this. We're not . . . that is, I mean, we aren't . . ." She stumbled to a halt, staring at the earrings as if mesmerized.

"Leya, I once asked you how I would know when you'd forgiven me for what happened in Oregon. If you wear those earrings, I'll have my answer."

Leya glanced uncertainly up from the contents of the box. "But, Court, they're for pierced ears. I can't wear them," she hedged, feeling quite flustered.

"You can if you want to badly enough," he pointed out, the corner of his mouth lifting faintly.

"I . . . I suppose I could reset them onto a clip," she began, thoroughly unnerved. "I mean, assuming I do want us to start over . . . which I do, Court, you must know that!" she ended in a sudden burst of honesty.

"I'm not talking about starting over, honey," he said, voice deepening. "I'm talking about making a commitment. If you want me as the man in your life, the man you trust and want, you'll wear those earrings as they were meant to be worn."

She met his eyes in sudden understanding. "That's supposed to be the easy 'nonverbal' way out of my, er, situation?" she gasped, shocked.

He sucked in his breath, eyes gleaming as he reached out to cover one of her hands with his own. "Leya, I've known from the start that I had nothing with which to attract and hold you except myself. You don't need financial security, you're not consumed by loneliness, you're not a naturally clinging vine. You don't need or want any of the things the women I've known usually want. Like a fool I tried to forge a physical bond between us, hoping that would chain you to me. The night you told me you could give me everything but your trust I realized that chain would never be sufficient, either."

"Court, I . . . ." she floundered, not knowing what to say. Was he trying to tell her he loved her or only desired her? Whichever it was, there was no doubt but that he still wanted her surrender!

"I know you feel cornered," he went on deliberately, his fingertips stroking the back of her wrist in lazy circles. "But so do I. My instincts tell me to grab you and take you to bed. My intellect tells me that would probably ruin everything. I don't know how to break the impasse unless you'll tell me for certain that you can trust me and that someday you might be able to love me. I want a commitment from you, Leya, so that I can know for sure you're willing to put the past behind us."

"What sort of commitment are you going to offer in return, Court?" she whispered, knowing she was trembling.

"Anything you want, Leya," he told her evenly. "Name it."

His eyes drilled into her, waiting for her response. She tensed, her hand trembled under his. He felt it and closed his own fingers more tightly around hers.

"Honey, I'm not asking for an immediate answer. Think about it," he urged. Then his mouth relaxed slightly. "And think about how much easier it will be to show me how you feel rather than having to say the words!"

"Should I be reading 'surrender' for the word 'commitment'?" she asked pointedly.

He hesitated and Leya nodded grimly.

"I thought so. You're still thinking in those terms, aren't you, Court?"

He shut his eyes and then opened them to gaze fully into her accusing stare. "I need to know you're mine, Leya. I need to know your commitment to me is total. Perhaps that is asking for a surrender."

"Perhaps!"

"All right, then, it *is* asking for a surrender. But I've already said you can ask anything of me in return!"

"You want me that badly?" she whispered.

"I want you that badly."

And then he was calmly getting to his feet, shaking off the mood that had settled around the little cocktail table. "Ready for dinner?"

"Court, listen to me. About these earrings . . ."

"They're yours, Leya. Do with them what you want, but if you decide to wear them I'm going to take it as an act of . . . surrender. The end of hostilities." He smiled gently, taking her arm and leading her toward the dining room. "That's enough on that subject. Come have dinner with me and let me tell you about my hard day!"

"Court, this is ridiculous! I will not let you do this to me!"

"Feed you? But your brother assures me the steaks here are fantastic and I have a hunger for some blood-red meat!"

"I'm surprised you don't ruin your own appetite with comments like that!"

But she wound up having dinner with him, as she had known she would from the beginning of the evening. Actually, she reflected at one point as she chewed rare steak, it wasn't an unpleasant meal. Court talked only of casual things, making no mention of what lay between them like live ammunition. And, as she had been before, Leya was gradually absorbed back under the spell of the companionship that sprang up between them on occasions when they were not discussing their own relationship.

"About next Saturday," he said at one point, helping himself to the rest of her baked potato, which she showed signs of leaving. "I was thinking that a drive into the wine country might be nice."

"Over to Napa Valley? Well, I suppose . . ."

"I know you've probably done it a thousand times, living so close and all, but I haven't ever done the winery tour," he said persuasively.

"All right," she said, discovering she didn't want to argue. "We'll go."

He left her on her doorstep after dinner, his good-night kiss a restrained, gentlemanly caress that astonished Leya. She stood at the window and watched him drive off into the night, conscious of the green velvet box burning a hole in her jacket pocket. When the taillights had disappeared, she dropped the curtain into place and headed morosely toward the kitchen.

Why was it, she thought sadly as she checked the back door and turned off lights, that of all the men she had met, it was Court Tremayne who had the power to make her feel this way? Jangled, uncertain, filled with longing.

Snagging an unfinished novel from the coffee table, she climbed the stairs to her bedroom. She set the deceptively innocent green box on the nightstand and crawled under the covers a few minutes later.

But it was impossible to concentrate on the novel. Her gaze kept straying to the green box, and twice she picked it up to gaze at the emerald earrings inside. They truly were lovely things, she thought with a sigh. If she were to accept, what would she ask of Court in return? What did a man mean when he said "anything"?

When she finally struggled awake the next morning after a fitful night, the green box was the first thing she saw as she opened her eyes. It stood on the nightstand where she had left it, taunting and teasing and daring her. It was certainly a reflection of the man who had given it to her, she thought with a groan, pushing back the quilt.

And the fact that she was even considering getting her ears pierced told her a great deal about her present state of mind, Leya decided grimly.

Because it was a perfectly ridiculous thing to do! What could it possibly prove? She *had* to be in love to even consider such a thing!

But perhaps, just as she'd needed some proof that Court's interest in her extended beyond Brandon Security, he needed a symbolic commitment from her.

The thought made her catch her breath. Was Court really so unsure of her? He always seemed so confident, so much in control. Yet here he was asking her to do something as ridiculous as getting her ears pierced just to seal their relationship.

The little box continued to haunt her. Court's request was crazy, yet hadn't she behaved just as crazily when she'd grandly turned over her shares in Brandon to her brother?

Only a woman in love would take such a situation seriously, Leya told herself wryly several times a day. Only a woman in love . . .

She *was* in love. Why go on denying it to herself? She was not a coward, either. She could admit the truth, she decided staunchly. And the next move, silly as it was, was definitely up to her! She would have to take the risk of making a commitment or face the much graver risk of losing Court.

By Saturday morning, she had resigned herself to that fact, knew it with a sureness that defied argument. She had been in love since the weekend in Oregon.

And she knew that, compared to her feelings for Alex Harlow, this sensation was unique.

As she stepped out of a warm shower and rubbed herself briskly with the red towel, Leya acknowledged that there was no comparison between her feelings for Court and what she had experienced for a boy like Alex. Court was a man and he touched her elemental femininity in a way Alex never could have done. It was easy to take revenge on Alex. It had become impossible to exact it from Court.

Yet he was sure that she had done exactly that by denying him her trust, Leya reflected as she slowly dressed in jeans and a bright red top. But who had she been punishing with her refusal to say she trusted him?

Could it be that the punishment had been self-inflicted? She had been more angry at herself than him that morning when she had discovered the deception. Angry at her failure to see through the scheme; angry at her apparent stupidity.

She had told Court the truth when she said she hadn't plotted revenge. Instead she had kept telling herself she didn't trust him because she had wanted to keep the reminder of her lack of intelligence firmly fixed in front of her. She hadn't wanted to admit another man had made a fool of her.

He had created a weakness in her that she didn't relish acknowledging, even to herself. That night on the terrace when he'd backed up her revenge against Alex, she'd found herself wanting to abandon her defenses against Court. She'd been on the verge of accepting his offer of a truce when her brother had appeared on the scene and reminded her of the weakness in herself.

But the thought of admitting her love for a man who had made it clear he only felt desire was another assault on her pride. Court was right. That pride was a factor in the situation, a very big factor. Was she going to be too arrogant to confess her love for a man who had shown her the weakness he could create in her?

But Court had found a way around the necessary words, she remembered as she walked back into the bedroom brushing her long dark hair. She stood silently for a moment, staring at the dangerous green box.

The drive through the rich Napa Valley was exactly what she needed, Leya decided a couple of hours later as she set off on the winery tour with Court. It was pleasant to sit back in the depths of the expensive car and let the beguiling companionship overtake her. Court made no mention of the earrings or anything else that might add a note of tension. He had been the soul of restraint all week.

It was fun tasting the various products of the vintner's efforts and selecting bottles to purchase and take home. They argued good-naturedly over the merits of Chardonnays and Cabernets, bought cheese and sourdough bread, and picnicked at a scenic point overlooking acres of neatly trimmed vineyards. True, it was a little chilly to eat in the open, but there was something cozy and intimate about dropping crumbs on Court's leather upholstery.

They talked about wine, electronics, jewelry making, and business, everything, in short, except the state of their strange relationship. It was a very pleasant day, one of those days when Court felt "safe" to Leya.

They took the organized tour offered by one of the

larger establishments, exploring the huge cellars and delighting in the tangy scent of fermenting wine. Once, as the main party of tourists passed momentarily out of sight behind a huge redwood vat, Court reached out and dragged Leya close for a quick, hard kiss that took her breath away for an instant.

"Couldn't resist," he explained matter-of-factly when she blinked her surprise.

But later that night after an evening spent dining and dancing at an elegant restaurant secluded in the vineyards, Leya felt compelled to take Court's hand as he was about to leave her with grave politeness on her doorstep.

"Wait," she said impulsively. "There's something I want to show you."

He arched an eyebrow in inquiry, but said nothing as he followed her into the house. Without a word, she led him firmly toward the stairs and knew by the sudden tightening of his hand what he was thinking.

"No," she said, slanting a mischievous smile up at his suddenly urgent eyes. "We're making a right at the top of the stairs, not a left."

Left was the direction of her bedroom. She felt the humor in him as she determinedly guided him right and threw open a door at the end of the hall.

He shot her a quick look and then whistled soundlessly as he walked past her into the functionally designed interior.

"Quite a setup." He nodded approvingly as he scanned the workbench.

Leya relaxed slightly at his obvious appreciation of her jewelry workshop. She watched in anticipation as Court bent over the assortment of fine tools and delicate apparatus. Little glass boxes filled with thin wire, earring clips, and other odds and ends lined one end of the table. A collection of polished rocks was housed near it. Sheets of hammered metal were stacked nearby.

He smiled at her across the short distance separating them. "I can see you getting lost in here for hours at a time." He picked up one of the small tools lying on the end of the counter.

"It's a hobby," she said offhandedly, not wanting to fully admit just how much she was enjoying his interest.

"Why did you show me your secret hideout tonight?" he murmured deeply, setting down the tiny tool and walking slowly forward to stand in front of her.

"I don't know," she whispered honestly. "Perhaps because it was such a lovely day . . ."

"And perhaps because you instinctively wanted to show me how much we really do have in common?" he mused, cupping her face gently between his hands.

"I . . . I'm not sure why I did it. It was an impulse," she shrugged.

"Do you realize why today felt so good?"

"Why?"

"Because it felt like Oregon again," he told her softly.

Leya hesitated, knowing he was right.

"And I'm going to do my damnedest to create a lot more days just like this one," Court swore, bending to kiss her in a sweet, drugging way that made her want to bury herself in his arms.

But he didn't give her the chance. His leavetaking was warm, filled with sensual tension, but very restrained.

Exactly like the leavetaking of the next several nights, Leya thought in wry amusement as the week progressed. Court had established a truce, she had allowed him to do so, and he intended to maintain it.

The planning for the new branch of Brandon Books went beautifully during those days, with everything seeming to fall satisfyingly into place. And the nights were filled with a fairytale prince who was all grace and charm and restrained desire.

Leya knew she was being wooed, and she also knew Court was intending for the romance to have a thoroughly definite goal. But he carefully said nothing about that goal. It was only when she slipped dreamily into bed at night, and glanced at her nightstand to see if the green box was still there, that Leya allowed herself to remember the ending Court wanted.

It was over a dinner of curried lamb and green salad, which Leya had fixed on Sunday night, that Court made his announcement.

"I'm going to have to go back to the Valley tomorrow for a few days to wind up matters on a project I was finishing before I moved here," he said calmly.

"San José? Silicon Valley?"

"Right. I should be back in time for that party your brother is giving Friday night. You'll be there?"

"I hadn't heard about it," Leya shrugged, accustomed to her brother's offhand invitations. He would probably have called her the day of the party to invite her.

"But you'll be going?" Court persisted, helping himself to more chutney.

"Probably. Why?"

"Because I'll know where to come looking for you

when I get back into town, won't I?" he grinned. "I'd pick you up but I don't know what time I'll be back so I'll volunteer to drive you home, instead. That's always the more interesting part of the evening, anyway!"

Leya bared her teeth good-naturedly at him from across the table and he laughed.

There was no denying that the dreamlike quality of the days and evenings faded considerably when Court left town. Leya found herself eagerly awaiting the phone calls that came regularly after dinner.

"Are you sure you're not calling just to check up on my whereabouts?" she accused cheerfully on Tuesday night.

"Am I displaying a lack of subtlety again?" he sighed.

"A bit, but that's all right. Your phone calls are much better than television."

"Thanks!"

He told her how his work was going, asked about hers, and somehow it was nearly an hour before he hung up.

The green box was waiting in its usual place on the nightstand when Leya went to bed that night. She lay very still in the darkness for a long time, staring at it and remembering the warmth in Court's voice on the telephone.

She crawled back out of bed and reached for the extension phone. Deliberately, she dialed Cynthia's number.

"Cynthia, I have a personal question to ask you," Leya began carefully.

"At this hour of the night?"

"Does it hurt very much to have your ears pierced?"

There was a moment of dead silence on the other end of the line. "Are you serious?" Cynthia finally demanded, sounding as if she were smothering a laugh.

"Very."

"Going to do it?" Cynthia prodded.

"I . . . I think so."

"Tomorrow?"

"If I put it off any longer, I may never bring myself to do it!" Leya confessed.

"Okay, boss, tomorrow it is. There's a department store across from the store that does it free if you buy the earrings from them. I'll go with you and hold your hand."

"I've . . . I've already got the earrings," Leya said slowly, having regrets already. The commitment she was contemplating seemed very final. But something told her Court was strong enough to handle it. She smiled to herself at the thought. She *trusted* him to be able to handle it. She *trusted* him to know what he wanted, and he had told her he wanted her.

"Well, you can buy some more cheap ones from them, or I will, so we can get them to do the ear-piercing free," Cynthia said cheerfully.

"Thanks, Cynthia, for volunteering to go with me, I mean. But you haven't answered my question. Is it going to hurt?"

"Bring a bottle of wine down to the shop with you, Leya," Cynthia advised and hung up the phone.

The next day turned out to be one of those inexplicable workdays that is an absolute rush from the opening hour in the morning until closing. Leya and Cynthia, who came in at noon as scheduled, were swamped.

It wasn't until Cynthia finally was able to turn the "closed" sign over in the window that Leya was able to talk to her about the earrings. Wordlessly, she handed the paper bag containing the unopened bottle of wine to her assistant.

"Do you mind telling me," Cynthia asked, taking the wine from Leya's grasp and carrying it to the back of the shop where she dug out two paper cups, "what brought on this momentous decision? I thought you had a thing about the ridiculousness of piercing one's ears!"

"Cynthia, I think I've gone crazy. This will probably be like getting a tattoo. I'll wake up in the morning and regret it!"

"No, you won't," Cynthia assured her, laughing as she opened the wine and poured it into the paper cups. "You're going to love being able to wear delicate little earrings. And it will be much more comfortable. No clips to pinch your ears. With your love of jewelry, I'm surprised you haven't done it sooner! Here, take a nice, big swallow."

Leya took the offered cup and did as she was bid. "Are we going to down the whole bottle before we troop over to the jewelry counter at the department store?" she asked interestedly, her eyes lighting with humor.

"Nope. Some for now, some for after. That's the way I did it. Let's see these earrings you've got that have made you take this big step."

Leya silently drew forth the green velvet box and handed it to her friend.

"Ah!" Cynthia breathed a moment later. "I understand. They're beautiful, Leya. A gift from Court?"

"Yes." Leya bit her lip and took another sip of wine.

"He knew what he was doing. They match your eyes perfectly."

Leya peered over to look at the emeralds. "Do you really think so?" She found it oddly touching that Court had thought of her eyes when he'd made the purchase.

"Definitely. It can't be a coincidence. These stones were very carefully picked out," Cynthia declared with assurance, handing back the earrings. She searched Leya's face. "You're in love with him, aren't you?"

"Like I said, I think I've gone a little crazy."

"Same thing. Have another glass of wine and we'll get the bloody deed done!"

"Cynthia!"

Chapter Eleven

$\mathscr{F}$ riday morning, Keith remembered to invite Leya to his party.

"Can you come?" he demanded cheerfully of his sister. "Court will be there if he gets back into town on time."

"Is that supposed to be a lure?" she joked.

"Naturally. I figure you two will probably be panting to see each other after his absence, but I'm hoping you'll both come to the party."

"You don't think we're a little too old for your crowd?" Leya asked mockingly.

"Not since I moved into the staid business establishment. I figure the pair of you will fit in nicely."

"Poor little brother. Miss your disco floors?"

"Not since I discovered women go for that aura of power we businessmen have!"

Leya hung up the phone with a rude crash, her

fingers going absently to her earlobes as they frequently did now.

There was no point in worrying about it at this juncture, she told herself later that evening as she dressed for Keith's party. The decision had been made; the deed done. It remained only to try and carry off the official signing of the peace treaty with a certain amount of style and panache. And if Court Tremayne had an ounce of common sense, she added grimly, he wouldn't tease her about it. She wouldn't be responsible for her actions if he dared to mock her!

She chose the emerald-green dress deliberately, liking the way it went with the earrings that blazed like small green stars in her ears. Cynthia had been right about one thing: Leya did like the more delicate nature of pierced earrings. It opened up all sorts of new design possibilities, she decided, glancing in the mirror yet again. She still couldn't get used to the sight of them, though, or what this particular pair of earrings represented.

She told herself at first that the last-minute decision to wear her hair down was a whim and then admitted the truth. The long, dark tresses cascading past her ears and over her shoulders provided a shield for the emerald earrings. With a small forward motion of her head, they could be hidden entirely, at least until another small motion, such as turning her head, caused the hair to fall back.

On the drive across town to her brother's apartment, it occurred to her that there was no absolute guarantee Court would be able to get back in time for the party, although he'd seemed convinced he would. It would serve her right, she told herself as her humor surfaced, if she'd gone to all this trouble and then had no grand scene to play!

That thought and the excitement radiating through her veins put a glow in the silver-green eyes that could only be compared to the tiny emeralds in her ears as she knocked on the door of her brother's elegant townhouse apartment.

"The lady in green!" Keith grinned, opening the door an instant later and shepherding her inside. "You look quite ravishing tonight, sister dear. Can I guess why you're imitating an emerald?"

"A little too much green?" Leya groaned, glancing down the length of her long skirt.

"Not at all!" he assured her, following her into the living room, where a number of other people had already gathered. "The effect is terrific. Court will go crazy. What can I get you to drink? The usual?"

"That will be fine." She glanced around the room at the well-dressed, cheerful crowd. "You know, Keith, a year ago I wouldn't have been able to imagine you giving a party like this," she added in an admiring whisper.

"Upward mobility," he explained succinctly, splashing liquor over ice with casual flair. "You have to act like a success even if you haven't quite reached that point yet."

"You're really getting into this executive lifestyle, aren't you?" she teased, watching with wry interest as a lovely blonde detached herself from a group of people and made her way toward the bar. "Your date for the evening?" Leya added in a low tone.

"Haven't got one yet," Keith told her easily, sipping his whiskey. "But I suppose Janice here might do."

"I'll leave you to impress her with your aura of power." Tossing a smile at the advancing Janice, Leya made her way into the fringes of the crowd, searching out the people she knew and wondering how many here tonight had witnessed the dramatic exit she had made from her last party.

She was seized with a haste that would normally have surprised her. But tonight, as the nervous anticipation of Court's arrival began to mount, Leya hardly noticed the eager interest of several males in the crowd. She responded to it because the excitement in her needed some outlet and each new man on the scene was another object to absorb the energy that pulsed through her, lighting her eyes and curving her lips in a lazy, challenging invitation. More than once, she felt a stray hand unobtrusively come into contact with the sable hair as it swirled almost to her waist.

"Keith mentioned a sister," murmured a newcomer as Leya was handed a second drink by willing hands. "He forgot to mention the color of her eyes."

"An important omission?" she asked lightly, lifting dark lashes to give him the full benefit of the near-platinum green. The stranger was very good-looking, she decided clinically, and he had somehow managed to cut out the rest of her eager entourage. She glanced absently around and wondered how he'd done it. Somehow, she was isolated in a corner of the room, hemmed in by a potted plant on one side and the stranger on the other.

"Very important," the man assured her, dark eyes narrowing sardonically. "I have a weakness for green-eyed women, you see."

"Your weakness doesn't appear to have brought you

to ruin," Leya grinned recklessly, tilting her head to study the waving black hair and handsomely cut features. Deliberately, she allowed her gaze to travel politely over the expensive, buttery-soft suede sport jacket and black shirt worn with a rakish air.

"Most of the time I'm able to control it before too much damage is done," he agreed, holding up his left hand to demonstrate a ringless finger. Then he glanced at her own bare left hand. "Apparently, you've managed to steer clear of the trap, too?"

"So far," she agreed, eyes laughing up at him. Where was Court? Perhaps he wouldn't make it tonight, after all. On the other hand, how was she going to behave when he did get here? The tension had strung her nerves to a fine pitch. The earrings tingled in her lobes.

"Something tells me you and I have a lot in common."

"But your eyes aren't green," she protested.

"Are you going to hold that against me?" he complained softly, bending his head down in an attentive fashion and bracing one hand against the wall behind her. He smiled. "I promise you I have other attributes."

"Have you?" she inquired dryly, arching one brow. "Let me guess. Do you play tennis?"

"Excellently," he chuckled, dark eyes warming.

"Golf?"

"Near-par game every time!"

"Jog?"

"Every morning."

"And where's your favorite vacation spot?" she asked curiously, letting him mistake the teasing questions for genuine interest.

"Any place I can ski in the winter and sail in the summer. Do I pass?"

"I'm afraid you just flunked," she told him sadly. "I don't do any of those things." She looked up at him with laughing mournfulness.

"You prefer indoor sports?" His smile broadened seductively. "I have a talent for those, too."

"You're very accommodating."

"I do my best."

Leya parted her lips to make a flippant response and was suddenly aware of a change in the atmosphere of the room. The gathering excitement in her blossomed into full bloom, and she felt as if she were walking a glass-edged tightrope. Court was here. She knew it with every instinct in her body.

Affecting a casualness she was far from feeling, she allowed her gaze to sweep the large crowd until she focused on the door. Court stood there, talking to her brother. The tortoiseshell hair had been lightly ruffled by a chill evening breeze, and he was wearing the conservative gray suit he must have worn to his business meetings during the day. The coat had been discarded, probably left in the car, but the classic white shirt was still neatly buttoned and the dark tie in place.

Even as she glanced in his direction, the golden-brown eyes swung abruptly and pinned her from across the room. Leya was very conscious of the attentive dark-haired man leaning over her, trapping her in the corner of the room, and of the grim narrowing of Court's eyes before he turned his attention back to Keith. Leya sighed. She would have a bit of explaining to do. Well, he couldn't expect her to attend a party and not mingle with a few guests, she thought righteously, beginning to edge out of the corner.

"Don't leave, green eyes. I haven't even gotten around to telling you my name," the man hovering over her complained softly, coaxingly. "And you haven't told me yours, either. Your brother forgot to mention that, too."

"My name is Leya," she told him idly, her eyes still on the door. "And I'm afraid I really must—"

"Hey, something wrong, Leya? Do you know the guy who just came in?"

"I know him. Look, if you'll excuse me—"

"My name," he said very distinctly, "is Alan. Alan West. Now about my expertise at indoor sports . . ."

Leya knew Court was starting toward her, pushing his way across the room. She couldn't see him now as the crowd came between them but she could feel the waves of his approach as surely as if they were made of water. They lapped against her skin in increasing frequency and power. She knew she had to get away from Alan West.

But even as she tried to dodge politely aside, Alan's hand fell protestingly on her shoulder. It did so just as Court emerged beside them.

"Good evening, Leya." His voice was a dark and unbelievably soft menace. "Say goodnight. We're leaving." His eyes went to the hand on her shoulder, and Leya stared at him unhappily.

Alan, sensing the suddenly thick atmosphere, took one look at the strained faces of the other two and removed his hand with a small exclamation of apology.

"Sorry," he murmured laconically to Court. "Didn't realize she was private property."

"She's having a little trouble understanding that herself, apparently," Court shot back coolly, grasping Leya's wrist and starting back toward the door.

"Take your hands off me!" Leya hissed waspishly as she was dragged forcefully through the crowd. "There's nothing for you to be upset about! I was merely chatting with Alan—"

"Flirting is the word," he growled stonily. "Did you bring a coat?"

"No."

"Good, then we don't need to delay any longer."

"My brother—"

"—Won't miss us."

"Court, I won't be dragged out of another party like this!"

"So sue me!"

"Damn it, Court—"

"What the hell did you think you were doing in that corner, anyway? Making comparisons? Or did you want to see what I'd do when I saw you? You once said something about being interested in genuine male jealousy, didn't you?"

"That's ridiculous!" she grated, a little frightened now.

"I agree. But since you're so interested, I'll be happy to show you what it's like to be standing under a ton of bricks when they come tumbling down!"

He turned at the door, his hands tunneling under the cascade of her hair to circle her neck. The tortoiseshell eyes were blazing. "I won't have it, Leya. Do you understand me? I won't let you drag anyone else between us. There's only you and me, and I'm not going to let you muddy the waters. Eventually, we're going to settle—"

His words cut off as he drew in his breath with sudden sharpness. Leya realized with a pang of panic that the movement of his hands had brushed back the fall of dark hair, revealing the emerald earrings. She stiffened, able to think only that the moment wasn't turning out as she had planned. She was helpless to deny the significance of the jewelry.

"Leya!"

Court's voice was a hoarse growl in his throat. His fingers moved urgently on the nape of her neck. "Leya, my sweet shrew, why didn't you show me right away? My God! You're determined to drive me insane first, aren't you?"

He didn't wait for an answer, dragging her close and covering her mouth in a rough possession that made her gasp. Then he held her a few inches away, his face intent, his expression urgent and demanding.

"Tell me, Leya. Tell me what it is you're going to ask of me. I gave you the right to ask anything, remember? Anything!"

Leya met his flaming gaze and gathered all her courage in the palm of her hand.

"I'm . . . I'm asking for marriage, Court," she breathed.

For a split second, he looked absolutely stunned. It must be her imagination, she thought wildly as the expression vanished in the next instant. He started to say something, and then Keith's voice was behind them, cheerfully interrupting.

"Hey, you two! This is a proper executive party! None of that around here!"

"This is a special occasion, Keith," Court whispered huskily as his eyes roamed with golden heat over Leya's revealing face. "Your sister just got herself engaged. To me."

Keith took the news much more in stride than Leya did.

"Well, congratulations, sister! Of course, I can't pretend to be astounded. I was pretty certain that was the way it would end. After all . . ."

"Later, Keith," Court murmured thickly, gathering a trembling Leya close against him. "We were just leaving. I'm sure you'll understand."

"So soon?" Keith grinned, smiling into his sister's bemused eyes. "But it's such fun seeing Leya struck dumb!"

"Treasure the memory," Court advised. "I'm sure it won't happen often. Now, if you'll excuse us?"

Leya realized abruptly she wasn't the only one who was trembling. She could feel the fine tremor in Court's hand as he guided her purposefully through the door. As she pulled her chaotic thoughts back into focus, she was at last aware that the moment had shaken him as much as it had her.

"If you must, you must," Keith was saying philosophically. "I'll see you both later." He smiled directly at Court. "Take care of her, Tremayne. She's the only sister I've got."

"You have my word on it," Court vowed with deep assurance, his eyes still on Leya's face. "I'll take excellent care of her."

A second later, they were alone on the steps. Wordlessly, Court hurried his silent captive down the short path and across the street to where his car was parked.

He tucked her gently inside, then slid in beside her, turning to pull her close in the cold darkness.

"Let's go someplace very private and celebrate our engagement," he whispered as she buried her face against his chest. His hands stroked through the thick hair, pausing to touch the emeralds in her ears as if he couldn't quite believe they were there. "My God, Leya, you don't know what you've done to me tonight!"

"Did you . . . did you mean it, Court?" she said in a muffled voice, thrilling to the heat and strength of him as he held her close. "Are you really willing to marry me?"

"I said you could ask anything you wished of me, didn't I?"

She swallowed, not certain she should pursue that. "Are you still angry about Alan West?"

He sighed. "I can hardly blame the man for getting you off to himself. It's what I want to do every time I see you."

"You're being awfully noble about it!"

"Aren't I, though? Come home with me, Leya, and let me make love to you the way I've been aching to do since we first met!" he pleaded roughly, his lips in her hair and his hands moving tantalizingly along her back. "I want you so much, my little shrew!"

"Am I really a shrew, Court?" she asked, her body already responding to the need she could feel emanating from him.

"You can be anything you want to be," he told her magnanimously, "as long as you wear those emeralds in your ears!"

She could practically taste the lazy male triumph in

him. Leya had told him everything he wanted to know by wearing the earrings. But all she knew about his side of things was that he wanted her. Wanted her badly enough to marry her.

Well, it would have to be enough, she told herself stoutly. She trusted him. Completely. He would not talk of marriage unless he was fully prepared to commit himself. Love would come in time, she vowed with the full depths of her willpower. She would *make* it happen!

"Where are we going?" she asked as he firmly disentangled himself and turned the key in the ignition.

"I told you. Someplace where we can celebrate our engagement!" His gaze glittered through the surrounding darkness, reaching out to touch her in an almost physical way. Leya shivered in reaction, aware of the weakness assailing her limbs.

"My house?" she managed after a few minutes as she recognized the route.

"It's that stairway," he grinned, much pleased with himself. "So romantic."

"Court!" she flushed, the laughter somehow seeming appropriate mixed with the passion. It seemed right.

But she found little else to say as he parked the car in her drive, helped her out, and took the key from her hand. A moment later, she stepped through the door and turned to find him closing it behind them with a final-sounding clunk.

They stared at each other in silence, drinking in the need and desire that was fully mirrored in each other's eyes. The tension wafted around them, coiling tighter and tighter as the curious silence continued.

It was Leya who made the first tiny move to break it. Wide-eyed, she put her fingertips on the slubbed silk of his tie. An instant later, she was in his arms.

"Leya, my darling Leya! I've wanted you so badly!"

She speared her fingers through the brown and gold of his hair, luxuriating in the thickness of it as he crushed her close. His arms were under her hair, which swung loosely down her back, and she could sense the rising desire in his hard frame.

The essence of him filled her nostrils, tempted and warmed her on a primitive, very fundamental level. Once again, she touched the knot of his tie and slowly began undoing it.

"You used to talk in terms of golden chains," she reminded him throatily, her lips parting sensually as she worked gently on the tie.

"One of us will be on a chain by morning," he grated. "I'm no longer sure yet who will be chaining whom!"

"Does it matter?" she teased, pulling wantonly at the end of the tie and slipping it from around his neck.

"I'm past caring at the moment," he confided.

He bent, sweeping her into his arms, his eyes going to the swing of her hair as she was lifted high against his chest. And then he was striding toward the stairs, taking them steadily, purposefully.

As he climbed, Leya toyed with the buttons of his shirt, her eyes full of dreams and unspoken love. At the top of the stairs, Court turned toward her room and a moment later she was dumped lightly onto the bed.

"This is the way it should have been that night up in Oregon," he rasped, as he came down beside her, his solid weight sending waves of shimmering excitement throughout her body.

Her lashes drooped mysteriously, moving against her cheekbones with a pagan, inviting flutter that was as instinctive as it was unconscious.

"Tell me, Leya," he begged, his lips hovering over hers. She could feel the barely restrained desire in him and wondered at it. "It should be easy to give me the words now. Tell me there will be no more revenge!"

"I trust you, Court," she admitted, knowing what he wanted to hear and knowing, too, that she could tell him nothing less than the truth now. "It was myself I wasn't trusting. I didn't want to acknowledge I was so weak where you're concerned . . ."

"Damn it, Leya," he gritted. "If you're going to tell me that what you feel toward me is the same weakness you felt for Alex Harlow . . ."

"No!" she interrupted gently, her eyes shining. "That's not it at all, Court. Alex used me. I could never have forgiven that in a million years. But I believe now that your deception was only another Court Tremayne attempt to short-circuit the usual methods and get to the heart of the matter. I believe you're telling me the truth when you say you wanted me from the beginning."

"I did, I do! God, how I've wanted you!"

He was raining short, feathery kisses on her temple, her eyelids, and the emeralds in her ears. "I must have you tonight. I can't wait any longer!"

"Yes, Court," she whispered softly, lovingly as her hands slid beneath his shirt and began to knead the hard flesh she found there.

She felt his fingers on her zipper and then the emerald-green dress was tugged off with a swift, impatient movement. The coolness of the room touched her skin briefly as Court levered himself up to skim off his shirt and slacks. Unself-consciously naked beside her, he began removing the rest of her few garments more slowly, lingering to touch his lips to each new area exposed.

She trembled as he slid his fingers under the elastic edge of her brightly colored briefs, but it wasn't from the coolness of the room, it was from the rising heat in her loins. He felt her reaction and leaned over to first kiss and then gently nip her shoulder. A moment later, he had slid the briefs down to her ankles and she was as nude as he.

"I'm going to make love to you tonight until you can no longer even remember my stupid deception in Oregon," he swore. "Until you can't think of anything else except our future!"

She shivered at the urgency in his words and in his body. She wanted to tell him it was unnecessary to atone for the past, but knew it would have to be done with her physical response, not words. Now, finally, was not the time for words.

His hardness impinged on her softness as he pressed himself against her hips. He was seeking to be enveloped by her in the way men have always sought with the women they needed.

"Oh, Court!"

Her head twisted on the quilt as she pulled him closer. Her toes clenched and unclenched against the soft material beneath her feet.

He gave an inarticulate groan as his hand sought the

dampening, fiery heart of her desire, testing and probing. His touch made her gasp and one knee lifted in an agony of physical suspense.

"Leya, my wonderful Leya," he husked against her breast as first his lips and then his teeth circled each nipple.

Leya could say nothing more for a moment, reveling in the voluptuousness of the experience. Court's flame-igniting mouth traced delicate patterns on the hardened peaks of her breasts for a short time longer and then plunged to the soft valley between them. His fingers were arousing her to unbelievable heights, causing her hips to arch upward against his hand in delirious abandon.

"I want you, sweetheart," he gasped, his legs moving against hers, probing between her knees until she welcomed him.

"Ah!"

Her cry was soft, pleading, seductive. As if goaded by it and the small, quick breaths which betrayed her heightened desire, Court lifted himself, looming over her briefly before settling into the warm place he had made between her legs.

His body surged against hers, yet he held off from the final culmination of the embrace.

Instead, he used the intimate position to arouse her still further with threatening, teasing, unbearably exciting little movements that nearly drove her wild.

"Please, Court!" she begged, twisting to sink her nails into the hard muscles of his buttocks in an attempt to draw him closer and closer. His legs were tantalizingly rough against the smoothness of her inner thighs.

As if he was finding the softness of her as entrancing

as she found his own hardness, Court reached down to stroke her from thigh to knee.

"Like silk," he blazed. "Hot silk."

Her nails in his hips dug deeper as he found the pulse in her throat with his lips but still he refrained from taking her completely. She delighted in the groan of response her small punishment brought forth from deep in his chest.

"Do you think you can control me in this because you know how much I want you?" he rasped.

She opened her eyes to find his half-laughing, half-challenging, wholly inflamed gaze eating her.

"Show me how much you want me!" she commanded softly, her lashes lowering in heavy, feminine invitation.

Without warning, his fingers closed around the curve of her hip and she felt his nails lightly scoring the soft skin there.

"Oh!"

The cry was a small shriek of pain and pleasure as the exciting, erotic caress electrified her. With all her strength, she moved against him, feeling the crispness of his hair against her breasts. Her fingers raked the length of his ribs, pleading, cajoling, commanding.

"Leya! My maddening, passionate, irresistible Leya!"

He buried his mouth in the softness of her throat. Simultaneously, he gently seized her wrists, anchoring them on either side of her shoulders. Then, with the power and mastery that seemed an intrinsic part of him, he used his strength to hold her arching body still for a crucial instant.

"Court!"

His name was a broken sob of passion and need torn from her parted lips as he asserted himself against her and, at the same instant, surrendered to her.

There was a sharp sound of raw demand from him as he surged into a driving rhythm that carried her along in the way that a storm over the sea sweeps across the waves. All of Leya's senses were alive in that timeless moment.

As the storm they had created raged, Leya's hands scored the skin of Court's back in passionate intensity. It was an intensity she knew she would never feel with any other man, and it communicated itself to him. Her nails slid lower, digging into the strong thighs above her own and the tiny, sharp caresses she inflicted seemed to push him beyond all control. His mouth closed hotly on hers as if seeking to swallow the faint, choked moans that issued from far back in her throat.

Leya clung to him, having no other alternative but to let herself be absorbed by the intense claim he was making on her body. She felt him push to the depths of her femininity, taking everything as if he had a right to her. A right that didn't hinge on the trappings of engagements or wedding licenses but was somehow far more fundamental and savage.

She felt at once tamed and untamed, as if the man who was putting his brand on her sought not to restrain her but to chain her in such a way that her wildness would be released only by him.

Frantically, the love battle between them leaped forward to its ultimate conclusion, roiling both in its waves until neither could have escaped. But neither wanted to escape, and when the end came they reached for it with all the physical strength and mental will of two strong, healthy bodies and minds.

The deep, hoarse cries of mutual exultation would have left a listener wondering who had surrendered to whom. But in the depths of the huge brass bed, the participants in the small war were unconcerned.

Chapter Twelve

The remainder of the week passed in a confusion of plans, hastily contrived parties given by delighted friends, and early conclusions to every evening.

It was the early conclusions to the evenings that were making her a nervous wreck, Leya decided analytically on the morning of her marriage as she dressed in the wool suit she had bought for the ceremony. For a man like Court Tremayne, it just didn't seem natural. He was the kind who would have taken advantage of the availability of a fiancée. She would have bet money on it. So why had she spent every night of the past week alone in her bed?

His restraint was making her far more nervous than anything else could have done, she realized sadly. And underneath the bridal jitters lay her own sense of guilt.

It was she who had asked for marriage. She felt as if

she'd tricked him into this final commitment. Leya remembered the brief shock she'd seen in his face the night she'd made her demand at Keith's party. Nervously, she bit her lip as she automatically went about dressing.

Would he convince himself at the last minute that he didn't have to honor such an extreme demand? she wondered. Visions of being left at the altar crashed through her brain for the hundredth time. If he'd really wanted marriage, why hadn't he taken advantage of her surrender? Why had he held his passion in check since that fateful night of the party?

She shouldn't have pushed him into marrying her, she thought abstractedly. She shouldn't have taken him up on his offer to let her make any request she wanted in exchange for her own commitment.

The waves of guilt and nerves ebbed and flowed around her as she hurried through the last of the morning ritual. What if he simply didn't show up at the church? Could she really blame him if he decided she didn't have the right to this much? Why had she pushed him? Whatever had possessed her? But she'd asked for the one thing she wanted. Or thought she wanted.

Leya shook her head wistfully. It was like being granted a magic wish and making it too hastily. Only in retrospect was it clear she'd asked for the wrong thing. She should have begged for his love. Not marriage. What was marriage without a guarantee of love?

Well, there was nothing left but to carry on now, Leya told herself bracingly as she surveyed the demure skirt and short jacket of her outfit in the mirror. The suit was of a decidedly neutral color, perfect for a wedding that was to be held in the minister's office with only a few witnesses, or so Leya had thought when she chose it. Now, as she looked at the abnormally pale color of the garment, she realized she had wasted her money on something she would never again wear. The lack of assertiveness in the color annoyed her. It didn't attract any of her senses, and the result was irritating. Still, one could hardly wear flaming red to one's own wedding!

The long length of dark braid had been twisted into a formal knot at the nape of her neck and the only note of color obvious in the mirror was that of the emerald earrings and her silver-green eyes. Leya hesitated over her jewelry box and then decided against adding anything else to her attire. She looked exactly as she felt: not quite herself. So be it.

The knocking on the door downstairs pulled her out of her reverie and, pausing to slide her stockinged feet into a cream-colored pair of heels, Leya headed for the stairs.

"Leya! You look beautiful!" Cynthia announced appreciatively, stepping inside and surveying her boss affectionately.

"Why do people always say that to brides?" Leya grumbled, not feeling beautiful at all.

"Because it's the truth. Brides always look beautiful!" Cynthia grinned, following Leya into the living room.

"You really think I look okay?" Leya's voice held a good portion of the skepticism she was feeling as she searched for her purse.

"Have I ever lied to you?" Cynthia demanded.

"Yes! The day you told me it wouldn't hurt to have my ears pierced!"

"I never came straight out and said it wouldn't hurt! You should have had a clue when I poured two glasses of wine down your throat before taking you over to the department store!" Cynthia retorted righteously.

In spite of her precarious mood, Leya laughed. "And by the time I found out it wasn't completely painless, it was too late to quit. One ear had already been done!"

"It was worth it. The earrings are fabulous." Cynthia located Leya's purse in the corner of the couch. "Ready?"

"As ready as I'll ever be, I suppose. God! I wish my stomach weren't so nervous!"

"Court's is probably just as bad," Cynthia assured her, ushering Leya out the door. "Where's your suitcase?"

"Good grief! I almost forgot it!" Leya flew up the stairs to collect the luggage Court had instructed her to bring to the church.

"Still no clue on where you're going for the honeymoon?" Cynthia asked when she'd traipsed back down the stairs.

"No," Leya said, smiling privately. "But I think I can guess. I expect it will be a beach somewhere." Assuming there *was* a honeymoon!

"I like him, Leya. I have from the first. He's the kind of man who will take care of his woman." Cynthia's voice softened and Leya glanced at her wryly.

"I always thought I took pretty good care of myself," Leya mumbled, secretly pleased at her friend's approval.

"It will be good for you to have a man around this big house," Cynthia said diplomatically as they went down the steps to her car.

"Fine words from a woman who's been keeping poor Mark dangling for months," Leya chided.

"You'll be dancing at my wedding one of these days, never fear!"

The closer they got to the church the more grateful Leya was that Cynthia had volunteered to drive her there. She really was out of whack emotionally today, she decided, taking a grip on her reeling thoughts. But, dear God! What would she do if Court didn't show?

And then, quite suddenly, there he was waiting beside her brother on the steps. Leya sucked in her breath and wondered at her own fears. Of course, Court wouldn't stand her up. He had given her his word, hadn't he? What had she expected? She could *trust* him! She took a grip on her emotions as Cynthia parked the car. She would make it up to Court, she vowed silently. She would teach him to love her as much as she loved him.

The queasy feeling in her stomach died. This was what she wanted. She yearned to marry this man regardless of the risks. She would never have run the same risk with Alex Harlow, her instincts said. But with Court, it would be worth it. She would see to it that he wouldn't regret being forced into this.

For the first time in a week, Leya managed a serene, confident smile. One of her normal smiles, she realized. She was feeling a little more normal, a little more sure of herself at last. It was only as she reflected on her personal turmoil since meeting Court that it became clear how far she had strayed from the routine of her rational thought processes.

"I almost didn't recognize you," Court teased in a whisper as he reached her and took her hand in his.

"You expected me to wear orange or red?" she grinned.

"One never knows with you." He looked as if he liked it that way.

The wedding passed in a solemn blur. Leya repeated her vows in a soft, firm tone and listened as Court did the same. The large hand wrapped around hers was steady and solid feeling but his kiss at the end of the short ceremony was curiously remote.

But there was no time to analyze his brief, restrained embrace. As soon as the minister finished, Keith and Cynthia were crowding around to congratulate the new couple.

"I have to hand it to you, Leya," Keith grinned, hugging her. "You picked a damn good way of ensuring that Court doesn't go to work for a rival firm two years from now. Regardless of what he does when his contract is up, he'll have to keep in mind the bonds of family loyalty!"

"Don't give your sister the credit for this wedding," Court complained good-humoredly. "I worked my fingers to the bone getting her to the altar!"

"Poor dear, you must be exhausted!" Leya mocked, aware of the heat in her face.

"I am. I intend to spend a good portion of the next few days in bed, recovering!"

"Court!" The heat in Leya's cheeks went up several degrees.

"You'd better get me out of here before I say something I shouldn't," he instructed pleasantly. Already he was leading her down the steps of the church as Cynthia, Keith, and the minister trailed behind. "We'll be back first part of next week."

"Where are you going?" Cynthia demanded as Court handed his bride into the front seat of his car and checked to make sure the suitcase was in the trunk.

"For a nice leisurely drive up the coast, and then a nice leisurely couple of days at an inn I know in Oregon!" Court announced cheerfully. "Think you two can hold things together while we're gone?"

"For every day you spend on this honeymoon, I'm tacking on an extra day to the period of your contract," Keith warned.

"As far as I'm concerned," Cynthia declared, "you can stay away as long as you like. At this rate, I'm going to have the last of my school expenses paid well in advance!"

"What a pair of mercenaries!" Leya grinned as she turned to wave at her brother and her friend.

"Just old-fashioned businessfolk," Court told her as he pulled away from the curb.

"Court?"

"Umm?"

"Are we really going back to that inn in Oregon?"

"Yes."

She eyed his profile. "I have no objections. I mean, you know I love that coastline along there. But why that particular place?"

"Can't you guess?" he asked softly, flicking a short glance across the seat.

She hesitated. "We're going to start over? Go back to the beginning?"

"Not quite. I'm not that patient," he laughed.

The drive was comfortable and leisurely most of the way, although they ran into a lot of rain at several points en route. Court handled the bad weather with calm sureness, and by the time they had reached the isolated inn, it was almost sunset.

"If we hurry we can make it down to the beach to watch the sun disappear," he told her encouragingly as they checked into their room.

Ten minutes later, they had both changed into jeans and were wearing warm jackets for the small venture. Leya found herself inexplicably keyed up, as if now that the crisis of the wedding itself was past, some of her nervousness was returning. Firmly, she put the reaction aside, twining her fingers with Court's as he led her down the path to the rocky beach.

Surprisingly, they walked in silence for a time, allowing themselves to unwind. The winter sun sank quickly, though, and when it did the chill in the air increased rapidly.

Still they walked, and Leya let the elemental surroundings soothe her jangled but receptive senses. It was good to be back here with Court at her side.

And then, just as she fully relaxed and let herself absorb the pleasure of the moment, Court spoke, his voice a dark thread of sound in the evening shadows.

"What's wrong, Leya?" he asked carefully.

She lifted her head, startled at his perception. "Wrong?"

He gripped her hand in a small movement of impatience. "I know there's something bothering you. Don't deny it. I've told you before, we're very much alike. That means there's not much point in trying to hide things from each other. Tell me, please."

He stopped, turning to face her, his features an unexpectedly anguished mask. "What is it, Leya? Are you sorry you made the request that you did? Are you regretting our marriage already?"

She stood quietly under the weight of his hands on her shoulders and forced herself to tell him the truth. He was right. There could be only truth between them now.

"No," she whispered honestly. "I'm not regretting the marriage. But I think . . . I think I asked for the wrong thing . . ."

"The wrong thing!"

She nodded sadly. Tenderly, tremulously, her eyes full of love, she touched his cheek. "I should have asked for something much more important. Someday . . . someday, I will."

His fingers sank into her shoulders. "What's more important?" he bit out. "What do you wish you'd asked for?"

"Your love," she replied simply. "Someday, when you're ready, I will ask you for your love. Will you be able to give me that, Court?"

"My love!" The words were an explosion of sound between them. His eyes glittered in the darkness. "My love! Leya, you crazy little fool! I've loved you since that first weekend! You must have known that! Why else would I have given you the earrings?"

"Oh, Court," she breathed, her heart singing. "Why do you think I wore them? I love you, too. I think I have from the beginning." Her silver-green eyes gleamed in the fading light as she met his gaze. She made to move closer against him and was surprised when he held her away, his eyes searching her face anxiously.

"You love me?" he grated.

"Yes, Court."

"But you didn't think I loved you?" he persisted, as if unable to believe such stupidity.

"You never told me," she pointed out kindly, smiling. "All I knew for certain was that you wanted me."

"And on the basis of that, you were willing to risk marriage?"

"Or anything else you asked of me," she confessed.

He pulled her close then, warming her with his own body heat, his arms closed tightly around her. "Oh, Leya, Leya, I can't believe it. *I* was the one who was prepared to wait for your love. I was going to capitalize on the fact that you wanted me and then, finally, trusted me. I figured that sooner or later you'd see that what we have is something special, something precious. I thought that eventually you would respond to my love . . ." He hesitated, and then Leya heard the softly muttered oath.

"Damn!"

"Court!" she protested. "What's wrong?"

"I'm thinking of the time we wasted!"

She gave a little gurgle of laughter. "I hadn't noticed! It wasn't very long ago that we were standing exactly where we're standing now. I don't think you can honestly say that a great deal of time has been wasted!"

"Yes," he contradicted feelingly, "it has. We could have been married that first week!"

"Oh, Court," she whispered. "I'm sorry about all the misunderstandings. But for a time I couldn't think straight. I was so afraid . . ."

"Afraid that I saw you as some sort of conquest? It was never that way, Leya my love. Never! I am capable of getting my own way without going to such lengths as seducing the sister of the firm's owner!" He sounded mildly indignant.

"Yes, Court," she agreed meekly.

"I think I fell in love with you when I saw the way you laughed at me in that picture in Keith's office," he went on judiciously. "But I knew it for certain when I tracked you down to this inn and realized you were the only woman in the world I wanted to have with me when I went for a walk on the beach. I love you, darling Leya. Every inch of you from your sassy little tongue to your incredible response to me in bed. I'm going to love you for the rest of my life. We're so much alike, you and I."

"I suppose that was part of the problem."

"I kept telling you it was," he chuckled. "I knew you had to work your anger out of your system. If I'd been in your shoes, I'd have had to do the same. I thought I had it made the night you revenged yourself on Alex Harlow. If only your brother hadn't made his untimely entrance on the terrace!"

"I was angrier than ever at the thought of having been so weak as to nearly let you talk me into starting over. But I wanted to start again, Court. I wanted it with all my heart. If my brother hadn't shown up when he did, I wouldn't have been able to resist! But it was myself I was angry with, darling. I realized that finally. And it was myself I was hurting by not giving up the battle sooner."

"You're wrong there! I was the one who was hurt!" He groaned ruefully, squeezing her tightly against him. "I was so sure in the beginning that it was going to be easy to slide you neatly, simply into my bed after what we'd discovered here in Oregon. I knew you'd be angry when you found out about the deception, but I figured that if we'd made love by then, your anger couldn't last. I was a fool. I went about it all wrong!"

"Poor Court," she teased softly, lovingly. "You kept trying to short-cut things and I kept making it difficult!"

"I'm glad you appreciate what a little obstructionist you were!" he teased.

"Oh, I do. But it's probably been a good experience for you. Something tells me you've had everything far too much your own way in life!"

"No," he said with great certainty. "Until now I've never had the one thing a man really needs."

"What's that?"

"A woman who can't be bought. A woman who loves him in spite of his inability to handle her properly. A woman who trusts him enough to marry him, not even knowing for certain that he loves her."

"You didn't know for certain that I loved you," she noted gently. "Yet you were willing to marry me, anyway, and hope."

He sighed contentedly. "Like I said. We're a lot alike."

"I don't know about that," she protested laughingly. "You haven't behaved at all as I rather expected you to behave this past week. Somehow, I saw you as the type who would have moved right in with or without a ring."

His grin was a slash of white in the darkness. "The night I returned from San José and found you wearing those earrings, nothing could have kept me out of your bed. But after that I told myself that I had done enough short-cutting. It was time I gave you a proper court-ship."

She heard the pride at his own self-denial in his voice and chuckled. "A whole week of it," she murmured with blatantly false admiration.

"Stop making fun of me! You'll never know what it cost to try and do things right for a change!"

"Yes, Court," she said sweetly.

"But that's all behind us now," he continued with vast complacency. "Now we can lapse into the quiet, humdrum routine of the average married couple."

"You sound as if that has great appeal."

"It does. It seems to me I've been running around without much rest since the first day I learned your name!"

"Such exertion! But it hasn't been exactly easy on me, either!"

"We'll both appreciate the peace and quiet from now on."

His hands moved along the back of her jacket, settling on the curve of her hips and forcing her into gentle contact with his hard thighs.

"Come with me, my dearly beloved wife, and let's get dinner and some peace and quiet."

He threw an arm tightly around her shoulder, curving her against his side, and they started back toward the lights of the inn.

"Court?"

"What, honey?"

"Really love me?"

"With all my heart. Do you really love me?"

"With all my heart," she echoed blissfully.

Dinner came and went in a haze of candlelight and music, sparkling silver, and linen, but Leya couldn't remember later what she'd eaten. She remembered only the pleasure of being able to look across the table and let herself sink into the depths of a pair of gold-flecked eyes that watched her with a yearning hunger.

"The next step, following tradition," Court observed in a husky voice as he led her away from the table, "is to take you into that glass-walled room facing the ocean, find that little private alcove, and let you seduce me. There's just one problem."

"What's that?" She smiled invitingly. "You don't think I can handle it?"

"I think that we might not make it back up the stairs this time. You are filling my head and my senses like brandy this evening, sweet wife."

"It can't be much different from the effect you're having on me," she told him softly, aware of the fine tremor that went through him as he took her arm and headed toward the stairs.

At the door of their room, Leya suddenly smiled.

"What are you laughing at?" he asked indulgently, letting them inside the elegantly rustic bedroom.

"The fact that you got out of carrying me up that flight of stairs. Aren't you grateful? On the other hand, it would have kept you in practice . . ."

He shut the door and turned her into his arms, eyes all golden and warm.

"I would have carried you up a mountain if it had been necessary!"

"Greater love hath no man . . ."

"I'm glad you appreciate it. There was a time when I despaired of making you believe in my basically good intentions!"

"Did you ever really doubt me?" she teased.

"You had me quite terrified there for a while! Oh, Leya, I adore you!" His mouth covered hers in a kiss of curiously gentle passion. "I thought you were going to drive me crazy!" His hands undressed her lovingly.

"A woman likes to be sure," she murmured seductively, finding herself naked in his hands. Her words were a deliberate reminder of one of their first discussions.

"I was sure from the beginning. I don't know what took you so long!" He smiled, lifting her into his arms and settling her gently between the sheets. And then he was sliding in beside her, warm, with a shocking power that immediately inundated her already awash senses.

"Oh, Court," she moaned, going into his arms with an eagerness that seemed to please him enormously. "Love me, please love me!"

His fingers traced the line of her spine in a sensuous movement that made her arch like a cat. She shifted her legs unconsciously and then felt her ankle tucked beneath his foot as if he would hold her still. The small chaining sent a marvelously erotic shot of electricity out to her fingertips.

She felt him draw her close, so that the softness of her breasts was gently crushed against the rough maleness of his chest and the passion between them flowed back and forth, making first one and then the other the aggressor. Leya experienced the joy of being lovingly seduced by her husband and then the equally pleasurable thrill of seducing him. The constant trade-off carried an increasing emotional charge that intensified with each turn.

When Court's hands stroked the length of her inner thigh, Leya trembled, and he pulled her sprawling across his chest, her dark hair swirling against his skin. She held his face, showering tiny, desperate little kisses on his gold-and-brown hair, his eyelids, and the tips of his ears.

"You're a temptress," he growled, his hands fingering her waist and finding the line of her ribs.

"It's your fault for tempting me first," she husked, her lips on his strong throat.

"Always arguing," he groaned hoarsely. "Even in bed!"

She felt the humor combined with the desire in him and knew that it would always be thus with them, a unique and loving blend that neither would ever want to lose.

"But a man has to exert himself on occasion," he continued on a note of seductive menace, pushing her flat on the bed and lowering himself gently, completely into her welcoming embrace. "And I want you so much, sweet Leya."

His desire could be no greater than her own, she thought dizzily, and was on the verge of telling him so, when his body claimed hers with a thorough mastery that made it impossible to speak. She told him with her response, giving all of herself and receiving everything of him in return.

The pattern of their lovemaking soared, making them one with the night storm that was rolling in off the ocean. The pounding of the rain against the window was in tune with the pounding of their blood, and the force of the gale set the primitive rhythm of their bodies.

And then, with a fierce cry that was muffled by the silky skin of her breast, Court reached down to clasp her hips, drawing her emphatically closer, losing himself in her softness as the end of their inner storm approached.

Leya's fingers clutched at the hard, muscled power of his back, and with a sobbing cry she surrendered to the impact of the tempest. She felt him being pulled into the vortex with her, and together they clung, riding out the winds.

Some time later, Court palmed the pink tip of Leya's gently curving breast and smiled down into her contented, gleaming eyes. He was propped on his elbow, his legs tangled with hers.

"Happy, Mrs. Tremayne?"

"Deliriously so, Mr. Tremayne."

"You're such an untamed little thing in bed," he laughed delightedly. "Do you realize that?"

"You don't mind the exercise?"

"Now what do you think?" He grinned.

"I think," Leya said laughingly, "that we're both much more energetic than we gave ourselves credit for!"

"You could be right. Personally," he drawled deeply, "I'm not too concerned about it now that I know the chain is in place!"

"What happened to all that humility down on the beach?" she demanded, running her fingers through his ruffled hair and smiling up at him with teasing green eyes. "You're starting to talk about golden chains again. Is the old Court resurfacing?"

"I know now that you love me and I love you. That does give me a certain amount of confidence," he said blandly.

"Egotist!"

"But look at the bright side," he urged helpfully. "You've got the same set of facts in your possession. And I always did think you were a reasonably bright girl . . ."

"Meaning?"

"Meaning you were the one who once told me chains work both ways. Whoever holds the links is as much a captive as the one on the other end."

"I won't ask you which of us is on which end," Leya said diplomatically. "Just promise me you won't let go of your end and I'll promise to hang onto mine!"

"It's a deal."

He bent his head and sealed the bargain with a kiss.